The Art of Overthinking

Ellen Zheng

CHAPTER 1

When I was a little girl, my mom called me ugly. Instead of *I love you*, it was, *you're so ugly* and *I didn't give birth to you, I found you in a trashcan.* Then I started getting chubbier than the average Asian girl and the label became fat. *Pàng.* I still remember the day that word attacked me for the first time. Twirling around in my pale green dress with little pink roses, I was oblivious, unknowing that the next word out of my mother's mouth would impale me every time I looked at a mirror.

But now here I am, ten years later, checking over my outfit in the too honest mirror, and I know the feeling too well. I am bloated, even at six in the morning. Gosh, I wish I could return to those days in that green dress. But I can't, because once that three-letter word attaches itself to you, there is no escape.

So instead, I scrutinize my body and hate on every single stretch mark that isn't supposed to be there according to those glossy magazines and hate the way my stomach rolls over the waistband of my too tight jeans. I pull a sweatshirt over the top.

Of course, it wasn't just my mom's words that caused all of this. It was my grandparents grimacing at the sight of me on our annual trip back to China, my aunts and uncles recommending exercises to my parents, and nail ladies whispering loudly about how every American-Born-Chinese child is chubbier, snickering, and blaming it on McDonalds. And then, the comparisons started. From classrooms to supermarkets, all I can think is, *Why am I not as skinny as the girl in front of me was and gosh, my thighs are twice the size of hers.*

Now that I think about it, my mother's words caused the least harm. They were just my first introductions to that word.

I descend the slippery mahogany stairs, head drooped, in an outfit that I don't like, but at least I feel safe from my own insecurities.

Bird chirps and cold air–the kind that makes your nose hurt when you breathe in–greet me. It is my eleventh first day of school, and I only have one more until college.

College. The word alone is enough to make the oxygen seep out of my lungs.

Going to a competitive "Ivy League Feeder" in New York City ensures *Gossip Girl* comparisons, but unfortunately, my high school experience is nothing like *Gossip Girl*. Instead, it's stressed-out kids competing with each other for leadership positions and grades to decorate their already perfect resume.

I'm sure there are some parallels, but I'm too poor and unpopular to experience them. I'm kind of an outlier because my parents don't come from generational wealth and I'm not exceptionally smart, athletic, or talented. I'm just a painstakingly average girl with painstakingly enormous dreams. I'm pretty sure they were my parents' dreams first, but they were pushed onto me to the point that they've become mine too.

Since today is the first day of school, I reward myself with a visit to the only bakery in the neighborhood. Located in a dusty corner in front of the subway station, the bakery is tiny, dirty, and in major need of remodeling, but the pastries and coffee are heavenly.

The bells chime in silvery greeting when I pull open the door. What can I say? Bells are my biggest fan. Well, maybe they are everyone's biggest fans but I like to think that they like me the most.

The mustached man rearranging the treat display stares at me in annoyance. I stare back, mentally gesturing for him to get to the counter to take my order, but I don't say anything out loud. I'm not *that* confident.

After a few more seconds of an unasked-for staring contest, he asks gruffly, "What do you want?"

"A caramel cold brew and a chicken biscuit with mayo on the side please." I plaster a fake smile on my face.

He huffs in acknowledgement, swipes my debit card, and punches a button on a large machine. I don't even have time to daydream before he slams a brown paper bag and a plastic iced coffee-filled cup on the counter.

"Thanks." I get no response, but I find the rudeness endearing in a weird way.

The bells chime once again, but this time it is a bittersweet goodbye. "I will see you next time, I promise." I don't even have to look behind me to know that the mustached man is giving me a weird look.

On the subway station stairs, the resident homeless man sits with a coin jar strategically placed in front of him. Per routine, I drop a dollar in and give him a smile. But he ignores me, as usual. Oh well, it's the thought that counts.

The station is grimy and rustic due to years of bad maintenance and there's probably a rat scurrying through the tracks. I take note to stand at least 5 feet away from the yellow caution line. Hey, I watch the news and I'm not a fan of dark, scary places. Even more so when a train can run me over.

But I wouldn't trade this station for anything else. It's been with me since my atrociously blue braces and pimples phase in 6th grade. And I kind of despise change.

To appear less awkward, I scroll through my Instagram feed and bite the straw of my iced coffee. But it's a bad idea because the only thoughts in my head now are, "Why am I not as pretty and skinny?" and "Why don't I get that many likes?" And these thoughts always circle back to the thought above all thoughts, *"Gosh, I hate myself."*

Out of nowhere, I feel a light tap on my shoulder and a deep voice talks.

Jolted by surprise, my hand releases my iced latte. Like one of those slow-motion action shots, I watch helplessly as the lid bursts and spills all over the floor and over the stranger's nice shoes.

But of course, life switches back to regular speed at the worst moment, and I'm left to deal with the fall out.

"Oh, my goodness, I'm so sorry," I manage to splutter as I turn around to face a gray sweatshirt. My face is flushed and I avoid looking at his face while shoving crinkled napkins that I found at the bottom of my pastry bag at him.

"No, it's my fault I shouldn't have sneaked up behind you," he responds kindly, accepting my napkins. After a few more awkward minutes, I gather up the nerve to look at the owner of the voice.

A foot taller than me with eyes the color of the sky in a storm, this boy looks like he stepped right off the set of a teen rom-com. His dark hair is artfully messy and lies in locks over his forehead. No joke, this boy is crazy cute.

"I'm sorry about the coffee. Can I buy you a new one?" he offers, kindly accepting the napkins.

Unable to keep his gaze, my eyes drift to his now coffee-stained shoes. "Oh, my goodness, I'm so, so sorry," I ramble, my face warming up by the minute. "This is so embarrassing."

"Don't worry about it, I think the coffee stain makes the shoes cooler. Now it's art," his voice is light with humor. "But if you insist, you can make it up to me by letting me replace your coffee." I can feel him looking at me.

"You don't have to, it was totally my fault," I wince as I gather up the nerve to meet his eyes again.

"I insist—," he raises an eyebrow at me, wordlessly prompting for my name.

"Isla, but if you insist then sure," I tuck a piece of hair behind my ear. Hey, coffee is expensive and a cute guy buying me coffee is totally daydream material.

"I do, Isla." He grins. "And I'm Slater. Nice to formally meet you."

Oh. My. Gosh. My eyes fixate on his double dimples.

"We might have to do a rain check though, I have school," I somehow find the voice to say. But I don't know why I said that because he looks my age.

"Oh right, I forgot my question." He chuckles sheepishly. "Which train do you take to get to Alistair Cabot?"

"That's so funny. I go there, you can just follow me I guess," I say even though this is not funny at all. This is downright mortifying. I glance down at the stain on his shoes again, feeling another round of "I'm sorry" and "It's fine" rise through my throat.

Maybe I should learn how to drive just to avoid encounters like this one.

Then I think about angry drivers and shudder. *Never mind.*

"Thank you so much. I would've gotten lost without you." Charisma radiates off him like air conditioning in a heat wave. And of course, I melt.

I giggle into my hand. "Of course! Heads up we might get lost either way because I am awful at directions, even though I have been taking this train every day for five years." I mentally reprimand myself. *Why do I have to be such a rambler? He definitely thinks I'm weird now. Even I think I'm weird.*

But then I get a laugh in response and giddiness shoots up my veins until the high is everywhere.

A blur of steel and light whiplashes us with manufactured wind. "Well, this is our train." My eyes look everywhere but at him. I'm paranoid that if he sees me staring, he'll know just how attracted I am and try to find nice ways to reject me. I can't go through another rejection with my dignity intact.

Slater follows closely behind me and when we're on the grimy R train, the close distance remains as we hold onto the same cold, metal pole, hands fingertips away from touching.

My heart palpitates in my chest and I swear I can hear it in my ears. "Three more stops to go Isla, you got this," I whisper to myself.

If Slater can hear me, he doesn't acknowledge it. Instead, he attempts small talk for the rest of the train ride, but I can't give him anything but dry responses. Yes, I have a cute guy talking limit.

Somehow, I made it through the seemingly longer than usual train ride. My only consolation prize is the lullaby of honking taxi cars and the scent of street hot dogs.

There's a comfortable silence that blankets Slater and I on our stroll to school. It's nice to feel like silence isn't something to be dreaded for once. And before I know it, we're in front of round brown doors with 'Alistar Cabot School' in gold lettering.

I hold the heavy door open for him.

"Thanks." He perfectly smiles, showing off his perfect teeth which makes his perfect face even more perfect. It's not fair.

"No problem," the words rush out of my lips. "Um, yeah so, I'm going to go. Bye." Then I walk away as fast as my short legs can carry me. When I see Elise by my blue locker, a literal wave of relief hits me.

"Hey babe," Elise hugs me.

"Hey! Excited for classes?" I ask.

"You know it," Elise winks at me sarcastically. "Also, my mother was telling me some gossip about there being a new student in our year at Alistar Cabot and of course, I did a deep search on the internet. He's super cute," Elise squeezes my arm harder than I thought was humanly possible. A sinking feeling ricochets in my stomach.

Elise squeals, squeezing my arm in excitement. "Oh, my goodness. Isla look, that's him!"

Seeing Elise point to him confirms my suspicions. The new guy is in fact Slater. Behind my locker door, I take a too long glance at him.

"The rumors were right." Elise sighs, hugging her books to her chest in awe. "The new guy is so hot!"

"Come on silly, let's get to class," I tug Elise down the hallway, but I'm also in some kind of a daze.

Third period AP US History is when I get to see all of my friends. Raina pats the empty seat next to her and waves frantically at me. Elise is still gushing over Slater to anyone who would listen. This time, the person is Aisha.

Elise craves the thrill that comes with crushes. But when she gets them, she grows bored and dumps them. Even though the chase is Elise's favorite part, it never lasts long because people can't help but fall in love with pretty, blonde Elise. I'd be lying if I said I'm not upset that Slater is her next target. Because he'll fall. *They all do.*

Tuning Elise out, I turn to talk to make awkward small talk with the person on my other side.

"Hey Lucy, how was your weekend?"

"Fine." She shrugs.

"Well, I didn't do anything during mine, I miss summer alr–" her eyebrows are furrowed, like she's judging everything that comes out of my mouth. "Um well yeah, gosh can you believe we're juniors?"

"Yeah."

"Time has gone by so fast, like it's only a year until we have to fill out college applications." I ramble, but by the time I finish my sentence, she's facing the person on her other side, actually engaging in conversation.

Gosh Lucy never fails in making me feel stupid. But I do what I must because I'm scared of looking lonely.

Our teacher walks in, putting an end to the chatter. He fits into the male history teacher cliché a little too well with his black skinny jeans and square glasses. Hands cover mouths as muffled giggles ensue, and even Elise stops talking.

"Hi, guys. I'm Mr. Johnson and I'm your teacher. We are going to have so much fun with history this year," he cheers. "However, since this is an AP class, we have to jump right in. Today's lesson is on the discovery of the Americas."

Groans arise in the class.

"Yes, yes, I know. Blame the school," Mr. Johnson smiles. However, the class gives their unprecedented attention to the PowerPoint.

The day drones on and now I'm walking into yet another dim-lit AP classroom.

I notice Slater instantly. He sits in the back of the classroom with the other popular guys. Of course they inducted him into their group already.

With more vicarious online stalking, Elise discovers that Slater's last name is Wesbrook and that his parents are big shot executives. "Gosh, his name is so perfect," she squeals, placing her chin on her hand. I swear I can see stars in her eyes.

But of course, it's not just Elise. The whole classroom is openly staring at him, and a very, *very* miniscule part of me wants to brag that I met him first. I've even come up with a name for it, *The Slater Effect*. I distract myself by turning to Raina.

"Did your parents agree to the date with Prince Naveen?" I ask. Last Friday when we were at Beans, our favorite coffee shop, a cute, Prince Naveen look alike barista asked her out.

Raina is still gazing off into space and it's so obvious that she is stuck in her own thoughts. "Yeah, this Thursday," Raina mumbles.

"You better let me help you get ready!" I nudge Raina with my go-to mechanical pencil, a #7 lead, light sparkly green. It's weird that a pencil is one of the constants in my life.

"Us too," Aisha gestures at her and Elise who smiles in agreement.

Raina looks at us like we're stupid for asking. "Duh." And that is kind of the basis of our friendship...being there for each other in monumental moments.

By sixth period, I find out that I have gym class. With all freshmen.

Great.

But I can't even blame it on anyone else, because it's my own fault. I pushed back on taking electives, until my counselor subtly blackmailed me. I have to applaud him. It was kind of impressive how he dangled graduation above my nose. With my hand forced, I chose gym and art.

So, now I'm here, surrounded by people I don't know.

Then, a too-familiar figure makes his way across my field of vision.

"What in the rom-com?" I mutter to myself, trying to disappear behind some bleachers. An invisibility cloak would be so helpful right now.

He sees me, of course. I mean what did I expect? I watched enough movies to know what would happen next.

"Hey Isla," Slater's smile lights up his entire face, making his thunderstorm eyes crinkle. "Looks like we're the only juniors in this class."

Wow, isn't life just one crazy coincidence?

"Yay," I respond, offering him a weak smile in return. My heart is a whirlpool of conflicting emotions. And of course, he is in my art class too.

CHAPTER 2

It's a Thursday afternoon and I am sitting on the plush white rug in Raina's room with Precious, Raina's tiny, slightly vicious Pomeranian, on my lap. With the way Precious is growling at me right now, I can't help but think of how misleading this dog's name is. She should've been named Ferocious.

With music blasting out of speakers, Raina struts out of her closet every few minutes and spins around in an outfit for us to rate out of ten.

In a green sweater, leggings, and white sneakers, Raina strikes a pose.

"Cute, but not first date material so I'm going to rate it a four," Elise says.

"Basic," Aisha declares as she tucks a dreadlock behind her ear.

"It's a little plain, but I do like it...so, seven." I shrug.

"Well dang. I kind of liked this outfit." Raina frowns. "Oh well. Next outfit here we go." Raina changes outfits surprisingly

13

quickly and walks out in a flowery, lavender dress and sandals this time.

"I don't know who chose this but it's so extra. There's no way I'm wearing this," Raina protests, wearing a grumpy expression.

Aisha, Elise, and I wear matching slack jaws and even Precious barks in approval.

"There's no way you're not wearing this. You look fantastic. Naveen's jaw is going to drop and dislocate," Aisha pushes.

"His name isn't Naveen. It's Mark, and I don't think I would like that to happen. Especially not on my first date." Raina grimaces. "Heck, I wouldn't even know what to do. I would just stand there in shock."

"I have to agree with Aisha on this one. You look beyond gorgeous." I smile at her. I can't help but wish clothes could look even half that great on me.

"Give us a spin, queen," Elise hollers, recording Raina on Snapchat. Raina spins around slightly, her grumpy frown still staining her face.

Elise posts the video on her story. "Gosh, you're hot!"

"Naveen won't know what hit him," Aisha nods.

"His name is Mark, once again." Raina frowns while we push her into a spinning chair in the makeup room.

Elise gets to work applying warm orangish-brown shades onto Raina's eyelids, I curl her hair, and Aisha oversees lip gloss and highlighter. Precious sashays between our legs.

After loads of hairspray, lip gloss, and bad singing, the look is finished.

"I'm proud of us," I announce to Elise and Aisha.

"We should start charging for our services," Aisha takes a picture of Raina. "Just for reference of our artistry. Maybe I'll make an ad on Instagram or something. Wait no, you should do it, Elise, since you have like a bajillion followers."

"I do not have a bajillion followers. If you want to get specific, it's 293,458," Elise objects, but a smile stretches her face. After blowing up on TikTok for her looks multiple times, Elise is now a bona-fide influencer. In other words, she is *the* Pinterest girl that you get pose and outfit ideas from.

Raina pulls us all into a hug. "Holy cow, I almost didn't recognize myself. Thanks for making me look beautiful."

"Girl, you are beautiful, you're the canvas. All we did was accentuate your features a little bit," Elise grins, her green eyes twinkling.

"Aww stop, you're gonna make me cry, and I'm gonna mess up this beautiful work you guys did."

Aisha instantly starts fanning Raina's eyes with her hand. "Nope you're not messing up our masterpiece."

Elise snorts then slaps her hand over her mouth, which has us all on the floor cackling. The laughter only ends when Mark repeatedly rings the video doorbell. From Raina's phone, we see that he has roses in his hand.

"Oh my gosh, that is so cute. He bought you roses!" Elise squeals, jumping around.

"Girls, it's go time," I cheer and we scramble out Raina's white room door. Her parents are thankfully at work today so they don't have to experience our rowdiness.

"You better tell us what happens or else," Aisha cautions.

Raina laughs. "I'm offended that you think that I wouldn't. Anyways, I love you all."

Raina walks down the grand marble staircase and towards the double mahogany front door. Precious quickly tails her, excited about the chance to judge someone new.

"Walk faster! Your man is waiting" Aisha calls out, going as far as cupping her mouth to ensure that Raina had heard her.

Raina turns around at the door and glares at Aisha before opening the door to Mark.

"These are for you." Mark hands her the bouquet of roses in his hands. He sheepishly rubs the back of his neck.

Raina blushes and fidgets with her fingers. "I love flowers." She turns to look at us and motions for a vase.

There's an adorably awkward energy in the air, and it brings the biggest smile onto my face. The joys of young romance, Then I get sad because I don't think I'll ever experience this.

Elise searches around for a vase in the kitchen cabinet. She finds a horribly orange vase with several weird patterns. Raina grimaces. The vase was *that* ugly.

"Sorry, I couldn't find any other vase," Elise says while Raina practically shoves the flowers into her hands. Mark is still rubbing his neck.

"Um, did I thank you for the flowers already?" Raina asks.

"Yeah, but I don't mind. Thank you for your thank yous."

"Thank you for thanking me for my thank yous."

It's silent in the room while we attempt to comprehend whatever Raina just said. Even Precious ceases her barking.

"This is so awkward, sorry. You're my first date. I've never made it out of the talking stage before." Raina shifts her weight from one foot to the other.

"You're mine too," Mark mumbles, a shy smile tugging at his lips as he is finally able to meet Raina's eyes.

Aisha speaks up and breaks the recurring silence. "Well love birds, go on then and enjoy your dinner." She pushes Raina out the door and shuts the door on both of them.

There's a brief moment of silence before Raina yells, "You know this is my house, right?"

"Go on your date already," Aisha yells back.

"They grow up so fast." A tear escapes Elise's eye. "My goodness, we forgot to take a picture of both of them to send to Raina's parents."

"Elise, you're such a mom." I tease, shaking my head.

Two hours have passed since we sent Raina off on her date and we're still at Raina's house eating cheesy pizza, and throwing popcorn at the plasma TV screen. The wonderful thing about Mr. and Mrs. Ahuja was that they allowed us to stay over at their house anytime. So, we do and now we're in their large movie theater room yelling at the stupid main characters for not getting with each other already. *How pathetic.*

I'd like to think that I can tell when someone likes me. Of course, it hasn't happened yet but if it does one day, I'm sure I would be able to tell and not be oblivious like these dummies on the screen.

"You know, he's been playing a high school student for at least 10 years." Aisha points at the male lead.

I cross my arms and shake my head. "It's like they're trying to force unrealistic beauty standards on us. Most of the high schoolers I know don't have a freaking eight pack, clear skin, and straight, white teeth."

"Hollywood's way of making us all feel depressed," Elise agrees. I feel bad for staring at her a minute too long when she says this. What has Elise got to be depressed about? She literally looks like the actress on the screen. Guys practically throw their numbers at her when we go out. I know it's not fair for me to think like this, but I do.

"Do you guys want to have a movie binge tomorrow?" I ask.

"Sorry, we can't. It's Friday," Elise says like it explains everything. For some reason, Elise and Aisha are never available on Fridays.

"Why no–" I start to ask, but then the beeping of the opened door interrupts me.

"It's either Raina's back, Mr. and Mrs. Ahuja are home, or robbers," Aisha announces. "Let's go check it out."

It is Raina, with her shoes in her hands and the biggest smile on her face.

I lean over the railing of the stairs. "The date went that well?"

Her smile doesn't slip from her face once. "Yeah."

Aisha's hands are on her hips in a stance that freakishly resembles my mom's when she wants to clean my room. "Come upstairs and tell us the details already."

We gather on the rug, crisscrossed like kindergarteners waiting for story time.

"It was awkward at first." Raina glares directly at Aisha. "I blame you for that."

Aisha raises both of her hands in defense and pouts. "What are you talking about? I just made sure the both of you didn't miss your dinner reservation."

Raina rolls her eyes and continues her rundown. "So, we got into his car and drove to the restaurant and just made polite small talk. At this point I was thinking there's no way this whole date wouldn't be awkward but then we saw someone totally faceplant at the restaurant and started chuckling at the same time."

"No way, you bonded over people falling?" I giggle.

"Well, when you say it like that, we sound like horrible people. It totally changed the whole course of the date. We learned that we both enjoy videos of people falling on YouTube and then the conversation just bloomed naturally."

Elise covers her mouth to laugh. "Oh, my goodness."

"We're having another date the next time my parents agree." Raina's phone buzzes. "Look, this text is from him right now."

Raina shows us her phone. It says: Had fun on our date today. cannot wait for the next one ;)

"That's kind of adorable that he types out his winky faces instead of using emojis. Weird, but adorable," Aisha notes.

Aisha and Elise tell their own date stories. Now I'm the only person in the group who hasn't been anywhere near romantically involved with someone and I feel empty. I contemplate in silence, listen to their stories, and laugh when I'm supposed to.

I'm happy for Raina, truly. But I'm also really freaking jealous.

At home, hours of studying awaits me.

There's a thrill that comes with waiting until the last minute before studying. The fear of failing pushes you to remain awake at unreasonable hours, but sleep tugs at you, begging for you to finally give in. I never know what's going to happen next.

And it's this exact fear of getting a bad grade that has me up at five in the morning solving logarithms while Taylor Swift blasts in my uncomfortable wire earbuds.

My eyes are blurry and my right hand is numb from gripping a number two wooden pencil for too long, *but it's fine*. Pain is an inevitable byproduct of success. Or at least that's what everyone says.

And at six, my mind calculates the amount of sleep that I'm going to get, one hour and forty-five minutes now, and I keep telling myself that it's *fine*.

The next day, my dad makes the subway trip to the city to take me to lunch after school.

I find him waiting for me at the bustling bus station in front of Alistair Cabot. The air is thick with the scent of exhaust and roasted peanuts from a nearby vendor and commuters rush past with their coffee cups, hurried footsteps echoing on worn concrete.

"Hey, Baba," I call out, weaving through the crowd toward him.

"Isla." He smiles as he adjusts his glasses, like he's checking that it's actually me. "How was school?"

"Good, I had a math test," I whisper so that strangers on the street and other students won't hear me. My parents don't understand English well enough so we only speak to each other in Mandarin.

"Study hard and get good grades. You're so close to college applications. Only one more year! If you get into an Ivy, this is the type of life you'll be living." He points at the Park Avenue townhouses, their elegant facades lined with intricate wrought-iron balconies and glowing bay windows. "You won't ever have to worry about money. This is the kind of life I want for you."

"Okay, Baba. For a brief moment, with stars in my eyes, I dream about what this life would look like...yoga classes, fancy cars, pearls, and power suits. I want this life too.

"What do you want to eat?" he asks.

I open my phone to the directions of the restaurant that I had researched while on my procrastination break. I ended up pulling an all-nighter yesterday, but it's fine. It's always just fine. "How does pasta sound?"

"Let's do it. Lead the way."

With only two crosswalks, we arrive at the apartment storefront restaurant. There's a plethora of empty, outdoor tables but no waiter, so my dad takes a seat and I follow him.

Once we're settled a waiter appears. "Sorry, you can't sit there, that table is reserved, but we do have open tables inside."

"What?" My dad frowns.

The waiter repeats his statement, but my dad looks around, confused. Then the waiter repeats his words a third time, but my dad still doesn't understand. Face flushed so I translate for him quietly.

"Okay." My dad gets up from the chair and follows the waiter inside. Sometimes, I wish he made more of an effort to learn English. It shouldn't be that hard. Why can't he just take classes?

When my mom calls him in the middle of lunch, he answers and barks loud, rapid fire Chinese into the phone. The other customers stare at us.

I sink in my stiff-backed wooden chair and cover my face like it will make me invisible. All I want to do is disappear.

CHAPTER 3

"The greatest pieces of art have a purpose. There is a reason that they were created," Mrs. Katz drones on. According to the framed certificates on the wall, Mrs. Katz has been chosen for Art Teacher of the Year for five years straight. It would be impressive if she wasn't the only art teacher at the school.

We don't do art in art class. Instead, we get to hear Mrs. Katz ranting about her life and referencing art every once in a full moon.

"Oh, you've got to be kidding me, I just want to paint," Camila whispers to me. I hide my snicker behind my fist. Camila is what I would consider a school friend. We aren't super close, but we enjoy complaining to each other about art class.

"Did you hear that? We have an art project. We're going to do stuff in this class for once." Camila shakes me in excitement, and I almost fall out of the spinning bar stool. Yeah, I did not hear that.

"Wait, really? On what? Already? It's like the third week of school." My questions stumble over each other.

"We have to create and present a piece of art that defines the true meaning of something with a partner. It's an entire semester long!" She squeals. "No more listening to Linda Katz talk!"

A project for an entire semester? It seems excessive, especially for art class. But it was a way better alternative to Linda Katz' rants.

I feel people are watching me. "Oh, my goodness. Yay! Want to be my partner?" I lower my voice.

Camila side-eyes me. "You really didn't listen to a thing, did you?" Before letting me respond, she continues, "We got placed into groups based on our last names."

"Well, that's lastnameist. Did you happen to catch who I'm paired with." I pretend to be casual as I whip my head around to search for someone I don't even know.

Camila bursts out laughing. "You are such a mess. It's the tall dark-haired boy over there who looks like he could be a lead singer in a boyband." She gestures to Slater, smirking. "You are so lucky, he's so hot."

So that's why people were staring at me.

"Do I have to go over there?" I groan, covering my face as if it was going to help with anything.

"Nope, he's coming over."

She warns me a little too late because the next thing I hear is a voice I recognize all too well. "Hey, partner."

I turn around in my spinning chair to face him. "What's up? Ready to get this project crackalackin?" I reply before instantly grimacing. *Why did I just say that? Someone please get me out of here!* I cross my fingers and pray that he doesn't notice that I just used the term "crackalackin."

I know it doesn't work because even Camila, who is at least three feet away from me now, cringes and shoots me a wide-eyed stare.

Slater stares at me for a moment before bursting out laughing. "You're funny. I don't think I've ever heard anyone use that word before."

Instant embarrassment. "Didn't you know? I'm a secret standup comedian, don't tell anyone." Even more embarrassment. Why can't I just stop talking? Someone needs to zip my mouth shut and throw away the key. Not that the phrase makes sense. Why would you need a key with a zipper? Last time I checked, zippers don't have locks, but maybe I've just been using the wrong zippers.

"Your secret is safe with me, I promise." He holds out his pinky finger, which I reluctantly join my pinky with.

"Let's discuss this project. I didn't pay attention so I sure hope you did," I confess.

"Lucky for you, I did in fact pay attention."

"Spectacular." Oh my gosh, where is this new vocabulary even coming from? I've never used these words in my life.

"You know where we can discuss this project?"

"Where?"

"At a coffee shop because last time I checked I still owe you a coffee." He doesn't seem to notice my strong embarrassment.

"Or, we could discuss it now like everyone else is doing."

"That would work if the bell wasn't going to ring in a few seconds."

He is right, the bell rings five seconds after he finishes speaking. I counted.

"Wesbrook, ready to go?" Elliot, one of the popular basketball players, peeks into our art class. When he spots me, he nods a greeting.

"I'll be right there," Slater calls out. "See you at five today at the Starbucks near the mall." I don't even have a chance to reply before he walks out the door with Elliot.

A torn sheet of notebook paper is stuck inside my art pouch. Plucking it out, I find a neat scrawl of phone number digits written in black pen.

At least I am getting free coffee?

Slater is seriously messing up all my plans. All I wanted to do today was watch *Gilmore Girls* on Netflix, under fluffy blankets, and drink box mix hot chocolate with fake marshmallows. Instead, I'm at Raina's house because she lives closest to the Starbucks that Slater wants to meet at.

For such a chill person, Raina absolutely freaks out when I tell her who I have to meet later and forces me to tell her all the details.

"Oh my gosh, that sounds like a total love story. I know you're going to get married and live happily ever after. I mean come on, does your meet cute not sound like it came straight from those rom-coms that you love?" Raina places her chin on her hand and dreamily gazes at me.

I have to admit, the way we met was kind of cliché, but I doubt he likes me. *I don't even like myself.* And I won't bother trying because the moment he tells you he doesn't like you like that and that he was only being nice to you to get closer to your friend is soul crushing. I can't experience that again. *I refuse to experience that again.*

"We are not a love story. I know for a fact that he sees me as the weird girl he has to do an art project with."

Raina attempts to call my bluff before grabbing a gel nail kit, which I'm pretty sure that I gifted her for Christmas. She forces me to sit down and paints my nails a pretty *Cinderella* blue.

I raise one of my eyebrows. "Why are you painting my nails? It's not like he's going to stare at my hands." I pause. "Unless he has a hand fetish."

Raina chooses to ignore me. Before I know it, it's time for me to go to Starbucks. Raina insists on walking me there because "it's only a five-minute walk and I need the exercise."

"You better let me know what happens. No details left out or else," she threatens me once we're in front of Starbucks.

"What if I just don't go?" Every nerve in my body tingles, protesting against seeing him.

Raina shoots me a pointed stare. "Isla."

I groan. "Fine."

"Shoo." She flicks her wrists.

I glare at her on my way to the door.

Raina calls out to me. "Can I come with you? Not to stalk you or anything but just because I want iced coffee? I promise I will practically be invisible."

I roll my eyes and laugh. "Bye Raina. Get coffee somewhere else."

Raina walks away with a pout.

I text Slater. *I'm here.*

I order an iced caramel Frappuccino at the crowded counter. The employee who takes my order is very pretty, with purple streaks in her hair that not many could pull off, and I feel extra insecure. Why couldn't I look like that?

Before I can pay, a card is shoved in front of me. Shocked, I look behind me.

"You really need to stop surprising me. For the sake of my heart, please let me know when you're behind me." I turn around to Slater, who has changed into another sweatshirt. Not that I was staring intently at him and memorizing his outfit, or anything like that.

Okay fine, maybe I was.

"Hey, I promised you that I would pay for your coffee. And I promise that I will announce myself next time. Thank goodness you didn't have a coffee to drop and spill on my shoes today." He shows off his *very* prominent dimples.

"That was an accident," I splutter.

"I know, I just like making fun of you. You're cute when you blush."

"I'm not blushing." I lift my hands to check. *Crap, I am blushing.*

An employee calls out the messed-up Starbucks version of our names. Today, I'm Irene and Slater is Skater.

"What do you think we should do our project on?" I ask when we settle down at a table.

"I have no idea."

We're both silent. My mind goes blank when brainstorming so I just sit there stirring my drink. Surprisingly, an idea comes to me first mid-stir. "This might be a weird thing to do our project on but this is my only idea. What if we did it on the true meaning of fear?" I ask. Then the way too familiar feelings of doubt and insecurity circulate through me again. "I mean it's kind of basic so we totally don't have to do it."

"That's genius! We can face our fears and paint what we felt before facing that fear and how we feel after." I wish I could say that I didn't breathe a sigh of relief, and that I wasn't reliant on someone's approval but I can't.

"Yes! Looks like we got our project idea and it didn't even take that long." Smiling, I reach out for a high five. Before I can awkwardly lower my hand, Slater returns my high five.

"What fear of yours are we facing first?" Slater inquires.

I don't even have to think about it. "Heights, especially roller coasters."

"We can go to a carnival or one of those indoor amusement parks. Can someone say field trip?"

"Dang it. You love roller coasters, don't you?" I groan.

His smile widens. "Maybe?" He sips his drink. "And for my first fear, we can go to a hospital."

I wait for him to elaborate, but he doesn't so I leave it alone.

An awkward silence lies over us like a blanket and there's only two choices, talk or leave. My choice is to leave, of course. I'm nothing if not a person who quits when it gets hard. From ballet in elementary school to soccer in middle school to now, *nothing has changed.*

"Well looks like we got it all settled. See you on Monday!" I get up and wave to him.

"See you." He waves back. I can't stop myself from turning back to glance at him before I open the door. To my surprise, he's looking at me too. Slater shoots me a wink.

A smile remains on my face the whole walk back to Raina's house. Obviously, it was the freaking Slater Effect.

CHAPTER 4

The cold air from my mom's unwillingness to turn on the heat until the last-minute wakes me up. Hugging my warm, flower pattern cotton blankets closer to me, I sit up, tired, and groggy despite getting tons of sleep last night.

There are very few days when I actually feel awake. Maybe it's the caffeine addiction, maybe I have a mental illness, or maybe it's just being a teenager. I have no idea. I'm just tired all of the freaking time. And of course I talk about it all of the time. Most of my conversations start off, end with, or only consist of "I'm so tired."

My half-awake mind wanders off to the most embarrassing subject. A certain boy with tempest eyes. A part of me can't help but fantasize about what would happen if he liked me. I dream about cute dates where we hold hands and Instagram posts where he calls me some cute nickname in the caption. Then the reality of it all slaps me.

Truthfully, I don't think I want a boyfriend *that* bad. I just want to be able to relate to my friends and those high school movies for once.

A new text from Elise appears in our friend group chat. *hi besties. it's girls' day, if u have a plan CANCEL IT. let's go shopping ???*

I wait for one person to respond before I text back. *Yes!!!! I'm excited.*

And now I'm sitting on the light blue bench of a train to Herald Square, sporting a ridiculously puffy coat courtesy of my mom. A Taylor Swift song pounds through my earbuds and I "sing" along under my breath.

Not long after the song finishes, the female robotic voice announces, "This is 34-Herald Street Herald Square. Transfer is available to the D, F, M, N train. Stand clear of the closing doors, please."

Somehow, I find my way out of the labyrinth of people in the station. The sky is big and blue, and there is a mixture scent of marijuana and hot dogs in the air. It's feeling extra New York today.

My phone buzzes in my pocket.

Aisha: *btw we're at the McDonalds in Macy's lol*

Me: *THANKS!*

Clutching brown bags in their hands, my friends are stuck in deep conversation. I don't want to interrupt, so I linger by the entrance.

Aisha notices me and beckons me over. "Slothie, you look cute!"

Slothie has been Aisha's nickname for me since middle school after one lazy summer that I spent, slouched on the couch moving as little as possible. The nickname has stuck, and while it's not exactly my favorite thing ever, what can I do about it now?

"Thanks. So do you!" I smile.

The greetings cease, and I fade into oblivion as they change the conversation back to Raina's Mark, Elise's newest DM, and Aisha's on-and-off relationship. At least I can steal their French fries to comfort me.

"OMG, you guys. Elliot and Connor are here according to the Snap map." Elise zooms in on their Bitmojis which are coincidentally near ours. "You know what this means right?"

Aisha pipes up, "High possibility that Slater Wesbrook is here." Just the mention of his name gets my head spinning.

"Ding ding ding! Right answer," Elise squeals. "Let's go find them."

"Are we seriously going scavenger hunting for them?" I raise a brow.

"Yeah, that's kind of weird and stalker-ish." Raina frowns.

"Of course not. I'm not *that* desperate. I'm texting Connor and asking if they want to meet up." Elise quickly taps her long nails against her phone. I can't help but admire Elise. She knows exactly what she wants and how to get it.

"He said "yes", and suggested bowling at his house." Elise looks up from her phone. Of course he did. Connor has had a crush on Elise since freshman year.

"I don't think I've ever even been to a guy's house. Also, mom and dad would definitely not approve."

"What they don't know won't kill them, Slothie." Aisha winks, and playfully punches my arm.

"Yeah, live a little," Elise adds. "Apparently, they were only at Macy's to pick up something for Slater's mom. We were right ladies. Slater Wesbrook is totally with them."

I feel a sliver of annoyance at their blatant disregarding of my feelings, but maybe I'm just too sensitive.

"Don't worry, I haven't been to a guy's house either," Raina whispers to me. I smile at her attempt at reassurance. "Isn't today supposed to be girls' day?" Raina addresses the whole group.

"I mean yeah, but think about it, we're hanging out with each other right now so girls' day is kind of complete. Besides, cute boys are totally worth ending girls' day early for," Elise says.

"Absolutely," Aisha agrees.

And it's two versus two with Elise and Aisha winning by sheer will, as usual. They're always the deciding vote, and there will never be space for disagreement.

The boys show up twenty minutes later, each in some variation of a sweatshirt and shorts.

"Hi, Elise," Connor says. Then he remembers the rest of us are here too, so he quickly adds, "Raina, Aisha, and Isla."

Elise smiles in acknowledgement but her eyes are focused on Slater.

I don't understand why Elise isn't even a bit interested in Connor, and I don't understand why Connor is still obsessed with Elise after years of rejection. But maybe that's because I'm too ugly to understand pretty people problems.

Aisha doesn't let silence occur for even a second and forces everyone in some odd conversation about animal shaped pillows.

I discreetly look at Slater from the corner of my eye. Unfortunately, he catches my glance and smirks, which makes me dart my eyes back to Elise. Guess I wasn't that discreet. Bummer, there goes a potential spy career.

And the odd thing is, he moves from his position at Elliot's side to stand next to me. It's not long before he says, "Hey, Isla."

I swear I can feel my heart beating out of my chest, running away, and never coming back. "Hi," I whisper, and my mind blanks. I forget normal greetings for a minute. "Umm, how has your day been?"

"It's been good. I really thought I was going to have an uneventful day, but then I got dragged to McDonalds by Connor."

"Sorry about that," I shrug sheepishly. What I really want to do is point at Elise and scream that it was her idea. Gosh, I'm a bad friend.

"Hey, I don't mind. I'm happy to be here." He bumps my shoulder with his. "Standing next to you and listening to our friends talk about animal pillows."

"The weirdest topic ever. I do have to say, they are cute and super comfy though." I laugh.

"What?"

"Come on, don't lie. Hello blushing penguin pillows?"

"Okay fine, you're right. But my question is why do they make it blush? I'm pretty sure animals can't blush."

"To make it even more cute and comfy. Duh," I deadpan, which makes Slater chuckle.

I'm so wrapped up in our conversation that I don't even notice that our friends had stopped talking and were staring at us. My face flusters. Animals may not be able to blush, but I certainly can. Before I can speak, Aisha comes to the rescue.

"Hey, new kid, tell us more about yourself," she says.

"Really put me on the spot like that?" Slater jokes. "In case you didn't know, my name is Slater Wesbrook and my favorite animal is a giraffe." He looks at me. "Wait, scratch that, penguins now."

I roll my eyes, but a smile makes its way onto my face anyways.

Elliot throws his head back and laughs. "Dude, look at you bringing back those kindergarten introductions." I think that's the most I've ever heard Elliot talk.

"The only thing I ever learned from kindergarten. Kid you not, I still can't color inside the lines," Slater says, ever so charismatic. The group giggles.

"But can we talk about how your favorite animal is a penguin?" Connor pipes up in an attempt to stir up laughter again.

"Penguins are super cute though," Elise says. "In fact, I think they're *my* favorite animal."

"You're right. Now that I think about it, penguins are my favorite animal too," Connor immediately agrees. Raina and I share a glance.

Connor spins his keys around his finger. "Okay um, let's go to my house!"

"Can I ride with you?" I elbow Raina.

"You know, a part of me wants to refuse and force you to spend time with Slater." Raina smirks.

I roll my eyes. "You are the absolute worst. I could also ask Aisha or Elise."

"Elise rode here with Aisha."

"Okay fine, then I can still ask Aisha and I don't think she would say no."

"I could make her say no."

"Please please please drive me." I give her my best pleading look.

Raina eventually gives in. "Fine." Puppy eyes have succeeded once again.

Connor unlocks his grand mahogany front door and pushes it open. "Welcome to my humble abode."

Humble abode it is not. The brownstone facing Central Park is gigantic with freaking statues at the entrance. Inside, the brownstone is a maze of opulence. The grand foyer is bathed in soft, golden light from crystal chandeliers that hang from the high, vaulted ceiling, casting intricate shadows on the polished marble floors. Rich mahogany paneling lines the walls, contrasting with the airy openness of the space. Ornate rugs, their deep reds and golds woven with intricate patterns, cover the floors, adding warmth to the cool, polished surfaces. If my mom was here, she'd make a joke about how our house looked like their doghouse and then remind me of the sacrifices she's making to send me to Alistair Cabot.

"Downstairs everyone. The bowling alley is in the basement." Connor points at the iron banister spiral staircase gleaming with gold accents, eyes remaining on Elise the whole time.

"So, Slater, right?" Elise asks like she hasn't memorized his full name by heart.

"Yeah," Slater says.

"What brings you to Alistair Cabot?" Elise plays with her hair and bats her freakishly long eyelashes.

"My old school wasn't challenging enough and Alistair Cabot provides so many opportunities."

Elise leans in close enough that he must get a big whiff of her citrusy perfume. "That's so cool." The eyelash batting is still going on. I wonder if it hurts her eyes.

"So, is everyone ready to go bowling? We should do teams to make it more fun," Connor deflects the conversation away from Slater. "Elise, you can be on my team."

"Um, sure," Elise answers, glancing at Slater and opening her freshly lip-glossed mouth.

Before she can speak, Connor cuts her off. "Aisha, you can also be on our team. Slater, Isla, Raina, and Elliot will be on the other team. You guys have more members, but I think my bowling skills will make up for it," Connor brags.

"In your dreams Cohen." Slater pats Connor on the back.

"I was going to go easy on you Wesbrook, but not anymore." Connor presses a button on the wall which makes a set of bowling pins appear. "You guys can get the first turn. The best go last, obviously."

"Dude, you are so full of yourself." Elliot snorts. "Can I go first?" He turns around to ask us.

"Of course, man," Slater does some kind of weird boy handshake with Elliot while Raina and I just nod and pretend like this isn't the first time Elliot has ever talked to us.

Elliot hits eight of the bowling pins in total on both his turns. Then Connor goes and makes a strike. Connor strikes a pose and yells, "That's how it's done!"

When it's my turn, the bowling ball flies behind me because I accidentally let it go too soon. In my redo, which I had to argue hard for, the ball goes out. I watch in disappointment as my ball makes its way down the gutter. The least it could've done was roll quicker, but no, it had to roll slowly and prolong my embarrassment.

Raina covers her mouth to hide her laughter and I shoot her a glare in response.

From the corner of my eye, I see Elise talking to Slater. About what, I will never know, but she's in her flirting stance with perfectly calculated touches on Slater's arm in perfectly timed intervals and perfectly batting her perfect eyes. Gosh, she's just so *infuriatingly* perfect.

"Isla, are you there?" Aisha waves her hand in my face.

"Yeah definitely."

"It's my turn."

"Okay."

"So could you please move?" Aisha asks, smiling.

"Oh my gosh. I'm so sorry. Yeah," I splutter. "I totally zoned out."

On the couch, Raina greets me with a bear hug.

Then it's Slater's turn, and of course he rolls a strike twice. When he finishes his turn, Elise appears immediately by his side, gushing over his bowling prowess.

"You're so great at bowling Slater. You're so hot Slater. Pick me Slater. I love you Slater. Will you marry me Slater?" Raina mocks in a high-pitched voice.

"Raina, that's so mean." I giggle.

She raises her arms in surrender. "I'm just re-enacting what is being presented in front of us."

That gets me cackling, which makes Raina cackle as well. Before long, we're reduced into fits of laughter on Connor's checkered floor.

"What's so funny?" Elise glances down at us.

"Bowling is a funny sport." Raina smiles innocently.

Elise shrugs, and turns her attention back to Slater.

It's the last turn of the game and our teams are tied. I feel bad for whoever's turn it is. They must feel the pressure too, because no one walks up to the bowling alley.

"Isla, it's your turn," Elliot says.

"You're messing with me."

Elliot shakes his head somberly. "It's your turn."

"Will anyone switch with me?" I ask, looking around.

"Nope, that's cheating," Connor yells. He mouths "easy dub" to his teammates. Jerk.

I groan, frowning as I drag my feet towards the alley. I lift the heavy bowling ball, curse whoever invented bowling, and release. To my disappointment, the ball rolls out.

"You got it Isla! You still have one more turn!" Raina cheers.

I form an apology towards my teammates, roll another stupid ball towards the stupid pins, and squeeze my eyes shut. Only when I hear celebrating do I open my eyes. The pins are all knocked down!

My entire team rushes to engulf me in a group hug.

"Atta girl!" Slater lifts me off the floor and spins me in circles, while Elliot repeatedly yells, "In your face," at Connor.

I try my best not to hyperventilate at the fact that Slater Wesbrook's arms are around me and that he's lifting me up like one of those characters in a romance movie.

My efforts are not successful.

Raina smirks.

CHAPTER 5

When I was a baby, my mom wanted to name me Island. She insisted that it was because she wanted me to be independent and beautiful, but I think she just liked beaches a little *too* much. Thankfully, Dad got her to settle for Isla, a slightly less peculiar name. But when she's mad, she'll call me Island Wu.

I blame my mom for a name that connotes loneliness. I know that my name isn't *technically* Island, but still.

The insinuation is enough.

Now loneliness and emptiness seep through every aspect of my life, even though I'm surrounded by people. I don't know who I would tell or if they'd even care, so I keep these icky emotions to myself.

But some days it's extra difficult to hide, and today is one of those days.

I hate that I can't even label it.

All I want to do is go home, curl in my bed, and soak in the feeling of nothingness. But instead, I'm at school, listening to

Mr. Johnson ramble on about the development of an American identity. The class does their fake, kissing-up-to-teachers laugh so I assume Mr. Johnson has made some type of corny history joke. The bell rings soon after and I catch the unfortunate keywords of "essay" and "Friday."

Gosh, why can't I get a break?

Besides, it's not like grades matter when all colleges want is *passion*. And of course, I have none.

And I'm running out of time to find one.

The lunchroom is crowded and noisy, and I can't find anyone that I recognize in the lunch line. Standing alone sucks when myriads of conversations are occurring around you. I'm the outsider, leeching on everyone else's joy.

Finally, I'm at the front of the line. I really want a chicken sandwich, but my mind obsesses over the number of calories. I settle for a salad and head towards my group's table near the bathroom.

We were all late to lunch because of a biology test in freshman year and it was the only table left with four seats. We've collectively agreed to remain there because of nostalgia, and the fact that every time we moved tables, something bad happened. The first time we attempted to move, Aisha spilled milk on a teacher. The second time, I dropped my lunch tray in the middle of the lunchroom. We happily remained at our little bathroom adjacent lunch table since.

"Finally, you're here, I was starting to get worried that people would see me as a loner who sits near bathrooms." Elise furrows her eyebrows. "Hello, cliché movie plot."

"Isla the superhero coming your way." She bursts into snickers. We're both aware that I am the furthest thing away from a superhero.

Aisha puts her tray down next to Elise, and Raina sits next to me. "Hey guys," Aisha smiles.

"That square pizza looks yummy," I joke. My words pour out monotonously, and I immediately regret speaking up. The emptiness still hasn't passed, and I can't even talk to my friends normally.

"Why can't they be normal and have triangle shaped pizzas? Square pizzas aren't pizzas." Aisha rolls her eyes while wearing a disgusted expression on her face. "They're just gross impersonators."

"So, you guys, I found Slater's Instagram but it's private," Elise frowns.

"Girl, what is the handle?" Aisha asks, eyes wide.

Elise shows us all her phone. I can't control my curiosity so I type his username into my search bar.

Life is seriously not fair. Even in his blurry profile picture, he's freakishly attractive. I hesitate for a second to overthink before pressing follow. Slater most likely won't follow me back, but the weird, stalkerish part of me wants to see all his posts.

Then I get the notification: **slaterwesbrook started following you. 1 minute ago.**

And I smile for the first time today.

"He followed you back, didn't he?" Raina grins and bumps her shoulder with mine.

"He followed all of us back," I state matter-of-factly.

"Yeah, but he followed you back first," Raina protests.

"Like that means anything."

"It means something," Raina says. "I know for a *fact* he likes you. Remember when he hugged you after bowling?"

I roll my eyes. "Raina, he was just happy we beat crap talking Connor."

"Whatever, Isla. I know what I saw."

Before I can object more, Elise frantically taps her long nails against the table. "We should go to his basketball game."

"He plays basketball?" Aisha asks wide-eyed. My eyes widen a little too. This is also news to me.

"Um yeah, do you guys not check sports rosters in your free time?" Elise asks. After some uncomfortable silence, Elise continues. "Well anyways, it's Wednesday and I think it would be fun if we all go."

"I'm fine with whatever, as long as we're getting ice cream," Aisha states.

"I have an essay to write." It's true, but I usually start my essays the day before it's due. I'm a procrastinator, I know.

"Pretty please." Elise attempts puppy eyes. Hey, that's my move that she is using on me! But I do fall for it anyway.

"You're going to bug me for the rest of my life if I don't agree, right?"

"Maybe." she smiles. I roll my eyes in response, but a smile appears on my lips. I kind of do want to see Slater play basketball.

"I'll ask my parents." I give up.

"Yay! How about you Raina?"

"Fine." She shoots me a pointed look and I pretend not to notice.

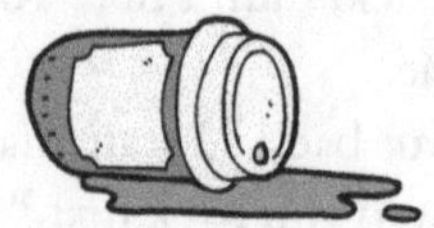

Mrs. Robins, my AP Literature teacher who loves rocking unique lip shades, a vibrant orange today, walks around the circular classroom and passes out bruised and battered copies of *Pride and Prejudice*. Mrs. Robins would probably call them "very loved" copies, though.

Pride and Prejudice is our reading for the month, and I'm excited. Jane Austen is a girlboss.

"Hey, Isla. Eat any dogs lately?" my assigned seat neighbor, Brent, chirps, and I remember why I dislike this class so much. Somehow the popular guys managed to get assigned seats together, but of course, I'm with freaking Brent. At least Raina's my other seat neighbor.

"Brent, stop being so racist." I roll my eyes. He's made comments like these since I've known him. The only difference is back then, I cared too much and would laugh along and agree with him. Then at home, I would cry into my pillow, wishing I was white.

I'd be lying if I said that I was completely indifferent to his comments now. I just know how to handle my emotions better.

"How is it racist? I'm just joking." Brent has the audacity to continue, "Want to do my math homework tonight?"

"Oh, my gosh. Shut up!" I am so not in the mood for his crap. Especially not today.

"Jeez, okay." Brent raises both his hands in surrender. "Females and their mood swings. She must be on her period." Brent mutters under his breath, like I can't hear him.

"Brent, choose a struggle. Racist or sexist? Or better yet, stop being such a bigoted idiot all together," I snap back.

He whistles. "Dang, feisty Isla. You know, you're kind of hot for an Asian. You're not a stick like the rest of them." Not only did he stereotype me once again but he also called me fat. Impressive.

Obviously, my words aren't going to help with anything so I just quietly seethe in my seat.

"So, everyone, we are going to do some popcorn reading because it's fun," Mrs. Robins announces. "Whoever wants to go first, raise your hand and volunteer."

Of course, Brent raises his hand first.

"Sure, Brent, go ahead," Mrs. Robins says.

He begins reading in an "Asian" accent, adding "ching chong," wherever he sees fit. All I want to do is run to the bathroom and cry, but then everyone would stare at me. I remain in my seat and clench my teeth.

"Brent, I think that's a little offensive," Mrs. Robbins finally interrupts.

"Sorry, Mrs. Robins. You know me, I just want to make everyone laugh." Brent smiles.

Someone speaks, but I don't know what and I don't know who. I can't focus.

All I want to do is scream that my race is not a joke, but instead, I betray *myself* with silence.

CHAPTER 6

Gym class sucks.

Especially when you're unathletic with a competitive streak, which is also the reason I'm walking up to the nurse's office with a severe nosebleed.

Thinking it was any other day, I changed into my gym clothes and walked into gym class. Coach Crosby announced that we were playing dodgeball and everything that could ever go wrong went wrong.

Coach Crosby chose two freshman male athletes to pick teams, and I was picked last, of course. Whoever invented the concept of team captains in gym class was sadistic. Letting people pick teams in front of the entire class is public humiliation.

Then Coach Crosby blew his whistle, leading to teenagers screaming and shoving each other in their conquest for colored dodgeballs. It was quite scary, really. Kind of like that scene in the Lion King where all of the animals were stampeding over Mufasa. I'm Mufasa in this scenario, by the way.

However, my secret inner competitiveness decided to also scream, scrambling for a colored ball. When I finally found a ball, I channeled my anger to throw it at the opposing team.

It didn't go well.

I don't have good aim, and I'm awfully bad at throwing in general. I watched my ball in defeat as it landed a good five feet away from me and I rethought my purpose in life.

Feeling air, I looked up to see something green hurling towards my face. The ball hit me right on the nose and knocked me on my butt with a thud.

The dodgeball game stopped and the attention of the entire class was directed towards me. Like literally, everyone was staring at me. As an introvert, it made me extremely uncomfortable. I mustered a smile, gestured for them to continue with their game, and ran to Coach Crosby for a nurse pass.

Seeing that blood was basically water-falling out of my nose, Coach Crosby begged me to go to the nurse. It would have been a hysterical sight if blood wasn't rapidly rushing down my nose.

Both hands covering my nose, I ran towards the door while everyone else watched in pin dropping silence. Yes, I was the main character, what about it?

Anyways, now here I am, finally arriving at the door of the nurse's office. The walk was weirdly long.

The nurse ushers me in and asks me what happened. After explaining my story, Lion King references and all, the nurse rolls her eyes and mutters under her breath, "It's always the gym students."

She feels up my nose. "Good news, it's not broken. But you took a pretty hard hit so I'm going to whip up some ice and you can stay here until your nose stops bleeding."

"Thank you."

Ziplock bag of ice in one hand and a tissue box in the other, I soak in the solace that is the elementary-kid-sized chair in the nurse's office. I don't think about anything. I just bleed in silence and shove a tissue up my nose every two minutes.

Unfortunately, my nose stops bleeding right when gym class ends and it appears that my presence is no longer welcome when I'm uninjured. Bummer, I thought the nurse and I were really starting to become close friends. We had quite a lovely exchange...I muttered something incomprehensible every so often, while she ignored me.

I strut into art class, holding onto my ice bag like it is a designer clutch. I could totally be a runway model for like medical tools or something. I can picture it already. The backdrop would be an operating room and famous models would walk behind me as I blow kisses at the adoring audience.

"Are you okay?" Slater asks once I sit down at our table. He avoids my eyes and twiddles his fingers.

There's no way he should be looking so uneasy unless...

I burst out laughing.

"You were the one who threw that ball weren't you?" I ask. This knowledge should have knocked out all of my attraction. But, unfortunately, it didn't. The attraction was very much still there, like my nose.

"I'm so sorry," he replies sheepishly, still not looking me in the eyes.

"You have good aim."

"Thanks."

"You should play sports."

"I do."

"You're paying for my nose job."

Smart guy didn't comment. He did, however, continue staring at me with guilty eyes.

I sigh. "I forgive you, okay? Now let's talk about our art project. I won't forgive you this easily if we get a bad grade." I punch his shoulder playfully. After getting no response, I began to feel self-conscious about my sense of humor so I continue talking, "So let's start on the project?"

He finally looks me in the eyes, but I kind of wish he didn't. Now I'm dizzy and I'm the one who has to look away. "Good idea."

"I know I have a habit of being right. Now go get us the paint." I shoo him away.

"Why am I getting the paint? Since I'm a feminist, I insist on you getting the paint." I roll my eyes and point at my nose, which makes him get up for the paint with no further arguments.

Slater returns with an armful of paint tubes. After noticing my stare, he shrugs, "I didn't know which colors to get so I got them all."

"Okay, Mr. Paint Hog."

"Hey, that's mean. I was anxious." He jokingly frowns. "The line for paint was really long and I didn't want to go back and get more paint so I got one of each color."

A giggle escapes from my lips. *Gosh, he's so adorable.*

I grab a sharpie from my pencil box and draw a line down the middle of the canvas. "My painting is going to go into the first box and yours is going to go in the second box," I gesture.

"Aye aye, captain. He salutes.

"Slater Wesbrook, you are such a nerd." I snort. I don't think I've ever laughed as much as I laugh around him.

But the happiness leaves as quickly as it arrives, and the empty, bottomless pit that I'm all too familiar with replaces it.

So, I paint. Color after color, stroke after stroke, line after line, until all the emptiness goes away.

But it never really does.

My mom stares me down. "Have you been working out?"

"No, Mama. Why?"

"I can tell. You should start. You're putting on weight." She looks me up and down. "Are you really wearing that? Your stomach is showing through the fabric."

My self-confidence is a statue, and my mom has just chiseled out another chunk. Tears pound on my eyelids, begging to be released, but I don't want to look weak in front of her. "Can you stop calling me *pàng*?"

"I'm looking out for you," She tucks a hair behind my ear. "You know I want the best for you."

"Whatever. Fine. I'll go change." I stomp up the stairs to throw another outfit in the "once I become skinny" bin.

When I walk down the stairs in a sweatshirt, she shrugs. "You look like a pumpkin, but I guess that's all you *can* wear."

"Well mom, you're fat, too." It's a lie, and she and I both know it. She's taller than me and skinnier than me. Even if I wanted to pretend otherwise, the numbers on the weight scale don't lie.

"That's why I'm watching what I eat. Something that you should do too." She frowns and I know that I've hit some nerve.

Me and my mom are warships, firing cannonballs of words at each other with no thought of the repercussions. I like to think that I sustain the most injuries, but neither of us ever truly wins.

The subway ride to Raina's house feels shorter than normal, and before long I can hear Elise shrill, "Toss me the mascara!"

Everyone is already on Raina's rug, and I'm the last to arrive, again.

"My bestie Isla is finally here!" Elise smiles, patting the spot on the rug next to her. "Sit with me."

I oblige. "Hey Elise."

"I didn't know that you knew Slater that well," she notes as she applies her mascara. Of course that's what she's asking me.

"Not really. We are just in a lot of classes together."

"Hmm." It's musical and pretty, and the last word she says to me. Elise makes you feel like the most special person in the world when she wants something from you, and invisible when she doesn't.

"Does anyone have glitter?" Elise asks.

Aisha throws Elise a small tube of yellow glitter. "Are you sure you want to use it, though? Glitter goes everywhere."

"I want to demonstrate my massive school spirit and support for our basketball team." She dabs glue and glitter onto each side of her face.

"That's a lie, you think basketball is boring, and you despise the mere idea of school spirit." Aisha isn't wrong.

"Maybe I just have school spirit for one of the basketball players." She winks at us. And of course, Raina is looking at me again.

I ignore her stare, and focus on my legs. My fat, stupid, thicker than my waist legs. My mom's words have left their mark, but it's no surprise.

"I would like you guys to know that ice cream is a priority, and I will be thinking about it throughout the game," Aisha says. "So, where are we going to eat ice cream?

"There's this ice cream shop that makes all their ice cream from scratch. It's super cute and aesthetic, and just a few blocks away from the school. I saw it on Instagram," Raina offers.

"Raina back at it again with the great store suggestions!" I reach for a high five which she quickly reciprocates.

After a good hour, we're finally ready. They're wearing white crop tops, while I'm in a sweatshirt. But due to Elise's persuasiveness, we all have yellow glitter on each side of our face.

"Mirror selfie!" Elise squeals, and we all join in and pose. "This is going on my Instagram story. We look so cute!"

"Don't forget to tag us because every time you do, we each gain like fifty followers. It's freaking awesome." Aisha peeks over Elise's shoulder.

"Are we all ready?" Raina asks.

We shout "yes" in unison.

Aisha stands on Raina's bed and mimics cheerleading moves. "Go—wait, what is our school mascot again?"

"Bears," Elise answers.

"Aisha, how did you forget what the school mascot is? They repeat it on morning announcements every morning." Raina laughs.

"I usually fall asleep during those." Aisha shrugs. "Oops."

"I'm so making fun of you for that," I say.

And finally, after another round of jokes, laughs, and "crap we're gonna be late", we're gathered in Betty's black leather seats. The game had already started, but Elise insists that it's better to be fashionably late than on time.

"Let's go cheer on our boys," Elise yells when we pull into the school parking lot.

"Elise, stop lying," Aisha jokes.

"Okay fine, one boy." Elise sticks her tongue out at Aisha.

The school gym on a Wednesday night appears way more intimidating than usual and I kind of want to just stay in the car.

Raina notices my hesitation. "Come on girl, let's go." Then she lowers her voice. "Do you really want Elise to steal your man? Especially when you look this hot?"

"First of all, he's not my man. I don't like him, he doesn't like me, and I never even look close to hot."

"But he doesn't belong with Elise, he belongs with you. Besides, are you really going to fail the rom-com community by not going out with him after a meet-cute?" Raina frowns. "And you're beautiful. You're the only one who can't see it."

I consider calling Raina on her bluff, but I settle on rolling my eyes. "You should focus all that attention on Mark."

"But me and Mark are great. In fact, our next date is Saturday." Raina smiles but then she turns to me again. "You and Slater on the other hand are nonexistent."

This leads me to another eye roll, but I let Raina pull me out of the car anyway.

The gym is packed, the air thick with the noise of excited chatter and the squeak of sneakers against the polished hardwood floor. The fluorescent lights overhead hum loudly, casting a harsh, clinical glow that makes everything feel too bright. We finally find navy bleacher seats near the student section, squeezed tightly between other students, their elbows jostling against mine. There's too many people, the lights are too bright, and I can barely hear myself think with all this noise.

I want to go home.

Elise squeezes my arm excitedly. "Look, Slater's number three."

My eyes glaze over the court, until they settle on the purple number three jersey. Elise is right. I can immediately tell that it's Slater by the way he carries himself. Slater Wesbrook radiates cool boy energy.

Someone passed him the ball and he's dribbling now. A defender from the other team is attempting to steal when Slater pauses and attempts a three-pointer.

Unsurprisingly, it goes in.

Elise stands up and shouts, "Go Slater!" She sits again. "Oh, my goodness, he doesn't suck at basketball! That makes him hotter."

Raina rolls her eyes. "Of course, he doesn't suck, he made the team."

"Yeah, but I didn't expect him to be *that* good."

After an hour of the ball being dribbled, passed around, and thrown, Elliot makes a tie-breaking dunk, ending the game 48-46 Bears.

Elise grabs my arm and drags me toward the basketball players walking out of the gym. We keep walking until Elise finds her culprit.

Slater puts down his water bottle when he sees us. "Isla, I didn't think I'd have the pleasure of seeing you here. Hey Elise."

"It's your lucky day." I shrug while Elise smiles and flutters her eyelashes. "Hey Slater."

"You looked great out there. You're like really good at basketball," Elise says.

"Thanks."

"You have very pretty eyes," Elise flirts. "Like, I swear I can get lost in them. I don't even know how to describe the color."
Stormy blue Elise, stormy blue.

"Thanks, according to my biology class, I got them from my mom through recessive genes."

"You're so funny." Elise bats her eyelashes while touching his arm. And that's my sign to get out of there!

I see some boys that I recognize so I wave to them. "Good game!"

They each thank me and offer me a sweaty high-five. I can't help but think that that's the second most interaction I've ever had with boys.

Before I can walk out of the gym, a sweatpants-clad Connor appears at my side.

"Hey, Isla," he says.

"Hey. I thought you played basketball."

"Nah, I'm more of a baseball guy." Of course he is. "Do you know where Elise is?"

"I think she's talking to Slater right now, but there she is." I point at Elise. "If you want to say hi."

"You're the best, Isla. Thanks." He practically runs towards Elise.

And of course, my attempt to exit the gym is blocked once again when my phone goes off. Surprisingly, it's a text from Slater.

Slater: *Please come rescue me. I'll owe you big time.*
Me: *You are so dramatic.*
Slater: *I'm begging you.*

I roll my eyes, but I give in. Maybe Slater will buy me a chocolate bar or something.

And it's some scene that I walk in on. Elise is flirting with Slater while Connor is flirting with Elise, and I almost get whiplash.

"Hey girl, ready to go?" I finally gather the nerve to cut in.

She pouts, looking at Slater wistfully. "So soon Can we stay a little bit longer, pretty please."

"Aisha wants her ice cream."

She wears a face of disappointment as she gazed at Slater. "See you at school?"

Slater and Connor respond simultaneously, "Sure." "Of course. Sad to see you go. I will text you?"

"Thank you," Slater mouths to me behind Elise's back, and I can't suppress my snicker. It is all just *so* peculiar.

Elise looks around. "What's so funny?"

"Nothing." She stares at me suspiciously, but eventually lets it go.

We spot Aisha and Raina by the exit.

"Ready to go get ice cream?" I ask.

"Do you even have to ask? I am starving." Aisha frowns. Jealousy claws at my mind. It's not fair that Aisha can eat whatever she wants while I get bloated just thinking about food.

Partygoers, dog walkers, lovers on a hand-locked stroll, joggers, and tourists crowd the candescent street. There is an undeniable charm to this city at night.

"He was such a good listener and he just let me ramble on. What a gentleman. It was really lovely, but then Connor butted in," Elise rants. "Connor is like obsessed with me or something."

"I don't understand why you won't give Connor a chance." I don't like how she treats him.

"There's a thin line between nice and weird, and he's on the weird side. If he stopped trying so hard, maybe I would give him a chance," Elise replies, eyes locked on her phone. "I gave Slater my number and told him to text me but he still hasn't."

"Maybe he doesn't like you?" Raina suggests.

Elise ponders for a minute. "No that can't be it."

A colorful sign that reads Eddie's Cones shines bright in front of us. Aisha squeals and scurries towards the door.

The contrast between Eddie's Cones and the city street is so severe that I have to take a step back. It's a pastel explosion, complete with pink booths and "love = ice cream" written in cursive on the wall.

"Isaac?" Aisha greets the curly haired boy working the pink counter. "I didn't know you worked here." Isaac and Aisha have been in an off and on relationship for three years. He is basically Justin to Aisha's Selena.

"Yeah, I started like 3 weeks ago." He smiles at Aisha. "You know when I first got this job all I could think about is how much you loved ice cream."

They both stare at each other for a way too long. I swear I can touch the tension.

"Can you stop staring at her and take our order already?" Elise interrupts. Last year, Isaac dumped Aisha by text and kissed another girl in front of her a few days later, and Elise has hated him since.

"Nice to see you're still rude." Isaac frowns.

"Is that a way to talk to paying customers? Maybe I'll let your manager know about your poor customer service." Elise smirks. Aisha widens her eyes and mouths at Elise to stop.

Isaac rolls his eyes. "What can I get for you guys today?" he asks in a fake, overly sweet voice.

"Strawberry for me, vanilla for Isla, mint chocolate chip for Raina, and you tell me what Aisha wants," Elise replies with her own fake voice.

"Chocolate?" he asks.

Elise laughs. "Aisha has always been a cookies and cream girl, but I guess you never paid attention to her enough to know that."

Isaac ignores her. "Twenty dollars and twenty-three cents."

Elise turns to us. "I got it." She whips out her debit card and writes two cents as the tip on the receipt while staring directly at Isaac. "It's a cent a day for how long you waited after breaking up with Aisha to kiss someone else."

Isaac is left speechless, Elise sashays towards a booth, and we mindlessly scuttle after her.

"That was amazing!" Raina says. "Can I be you when I grow up?"

Elise smiles, but doesn't say a thing.

"I love you so much for standing up for me, but I'm sorry, I'm weak." Aisha says, standing up.

"Aisha, no! You deserve so much better." Elise grabs onto Aisha's arm.

"But I can tell that he's changed," Aisha insists as she pulls away. Isaac is Aisha's *clutch*, and she'll go back whenever he wants her.

CHAPTER 7

Leg bouncing against the confines of my math desk, I track my precalculus teacher, Mr. Walter's movements around the room. The classroom feels cramped, with desks tightly arranged in rows beneath the harsh buzz of fluorescent lights. He promenades around, bestowing graded tests to his anxious subjects, the air thick with the scent of chalk and the faint hum of the overhead lights.

There's an incomparable high to getting your tests back. Especially when you felt good walking out of the test. But that might be because my parents have precisely engineered me to crave academic validation.

After more sauntering around, Mr. Walker finally places a flipped-over test on my desk. I turn it over immediately.

But instead of a high, it's a shock, because at the top of the paper in bright, dream-crushing red ink is "51%".

Crap.

My parents are going to freak out.

I'm freaking out.

My heart sinks, and it's becoming hard to breathe. I don't understand.

Why wasn't my effort enough?

Why am I not enough?

I stumble over red-ink marked pages, and my head spins so fast that everything becomes a blur. Then I reprimand my past self and pray for a time machine. But this isn't a sci-fi novel.

Here, time is a dandelion blown into the wind. Because of its initial abundance, you get cocky. And as the wisps escape into the sky, you admire the beauty of its flight, trusting that you'll always have more. But then everything disappears, and you're still stuck in the same place wondering, "Where did it all go?"

I sink back in the too familiar abyss of emptiness, and watch my dreams disappear with flicks of a red pen.

I'm not enough.

Not enough for an elite college, not enough for *anything*. I'm Isla Wu, the passionless girl with huge, impossible dreams. Maybe I needed this reality check to show me that all I'll ever be is a failure.

But it freaking sucks that I can't cry in class without embarrassing myself.

"I got a 98," Raina exclaims, and a few other people rush over to congratulate her. But I can't even try to feel happy for her. Envy takes over every *single* time.

"What'd you get Isla?" Raina asks, peeking at my test over my shoulder. I raise my paper to show her the grade, but the problem with that is anyone can look.

Behind me, someone whispers, "How did Isla get a 51? She's Asian. This test was so easy too." The class erupts into whispers and conspiracy theories.

Raina mouths, "Sorry," and leans over her chair to hug my side. I don't get why people say "I'm sorry" in response to failed tests. It only makes me feel worse.

But I pat her hand to let her know that I'm fine, even though I'm *definitely not*.

By this point, I realize that I've already caused enough commotion so I ask Mr. Walters if I can go to the bathroom. All eyes are on me like I'm an A-List celebrity walking down the street, and they're tracking my every movement to see what I will do next.

But they're disappointed because I'm not a reality star, but a person who deals with pain by overthinking, crying, and *just being alone*.

The train ride home flies by, and before I know it, I'm pacing back and forth on my doorstep. I'm scared to open the door, because I know the pain that awaits me. But the optimistic part of me hopes that maybe my parents will handle it okay and give me the support that I desperately crave. Maybe they'll understand for once.

Then reality laughs in my face.

But I suck it up and open the door because it's going to happen sometime today.

I find my parents lying on the leather couch, watching a C-drama on our too big TV.

"Isla, there you are." My mom beams. "Come sit." She scoots to the side and makes space for me between her and dad.

"How'd you do on your math test?" my dad asks. Of course that's the first thing he asks me.

The urge to lie entices me, but my parents would eventually find out because of an awful invention known as online grades. Then they'd get angrier because I lied to them.

"Fifty-one," I mumble.

"Ninety-nine? I knew it. That's why I cooked such a big feast tonight." My mom boasts. Well crap, she's got food involved and everything.

"Fifty-one," I repeat, and the pain sucker punches me in the gut. Why can't I get a break?

There's a period of silence before the yelling starts.

My mom's face is flushed and her teeth are clenched. "Island Wu, are you kidding me? After every sacrifice we make for you, you can't repay us by just studying and doing well on your tests?"

My dad doesn't speak but his eyebrows are furrowed in disappointment. And that silence speaks a million more words.

"I'm sorry," I whisper. Tears race down my cheek, and I can't stop them, even if I try.

"Sorry doesn't cut it." My mom glares. "It's your actions that matter. I guess that's our fault for spoiling you. You get lazy."

I heave with blurry eyes and a stuffy nose. "You think I wanted this?"

"Yes. Now you can fake those tears however you want, but I'm not a fool."

"I'm not faking. I'm genuinely upset." I'm upset about the extent that I tear myself apart just to make them happy and I'm upset that it'll never work. Despite how much of myself I give away and how hard I try, I will always be disappointing, Isla Wu. It's freaking inevitable.

"Go to your room. I can't even look at you right now," my dad finally says. True to his word, he doesn't spare me a glance. It's like I don't exist.

But it's not just them that's disappointed in me now. I'm disappointed in myself too. Disappointed that I flunked a test and disappointed that I thought, even for a second, that my parents would understand.

I sniffle up the stairs while my parents shout over my ruined future. When I finally reach my room, I check the online grade-book for the damage.

Fifteen. *Freaking*. Points.

Then I get on my bed, shove my face into a pillow, and cry some more.

I don't realize that I've fallen asleep until the ringing cry of FaceTime jolts me awake. Through squinched eyes, I make out Aisha, Elise, and Raina's name and press accept.

"Hi guys," I croak.

"Great you're here." Elise beams. "Now Aisha, tell us what happened."

Aisha's eyes are red. "He broke up with me over text. Again."

"Sorry babe." Elise hugs Aisha. "I don't understand why you keep going back. He might be cute, but no cute boy is worth crying over."

"I don't completely understand it either. It's like when he gives me even just a sliver of his attention, I feel like I'm on the top of the world. Then he changes his mind, and I plummet." She sighs. "But that tiny moment of happiness always seems to be worth the pain."

"Aisha, if I could give you a hug over the phone, I totally would," Raina says.

"Thanks." Aisha croaks. Besides bloodshot eyes, she doesn't show any signs of vulnerability.

However, I'm not as strong as Aisha, and I take my anger out on other people. "You know he's awful towards you and everyone else reminds you. You could easily find someone else that makes you just as happy, but you just love getting your heart broken, don't you?"

Elise's eyes are wide open. "Goodness Isla, that's harsh."

But I can't stop the flooding gate that is my mouth. "Someone has to give her a reality check. She can't forever live in dream world, imagining Isaac as Prince Charming, thinking that she will change him and then they'll ride off in a carriage to happily ever after. Let's be realistic!"

Even Raina is shaking her head now, and the guilt explodes over me, supernova style.

"I'm sorry." I slap my hands over my mouth. "I'm taking all my hurt out on you and that's totally unfair."

"Isla, don't worry, you're right. It's extremely painful to hear now, but everything you're saying is true," Aisha reassures me. "But I do need to hang up because I just need some alone time."

What is wrong with me?

CHAPTER 8

After a weekend of crying, I accept that life still has to go on. I swear to myself that I will rock the next test, and begin to feel better. And by better, I mean not being on the verge of tears every second.

However, grades aren't my only worry. My parents are a scary combo of disappointment and anger, and my friends, maybe ex-friends now, definitely hate me.

But of course, the minute I walk into school, I spot them crowded around me and Elise's lockers. I take a deep breath, which doesn't do anything, and face the weather. "Hey guys."

When everyone greets me back, I'm emboldened to turn to Aisha. "I'm so sorry about my outburst. I was taking my anger out on you which is so not okay."

"Slothie, babe, don't stress. You were just being a good friend and looking out for me." She smiles her mega-kilowatt smile.

Yeah, it definitely wasn't that. However, I return a tight-lipped smile and focus on opening my locker. The difficult lock leaves me with battle scars on my finger pads.

"Are your parents still mad?" Raina asks.

"Yeah." I shrug. "My dad still won't talk to me, and whenever my mom sees me, she starts yelling."

Raina looks at me with pity. "It's totally not fair. One bad test grade won't ruin your life."

"Tell that to my parents." I slam my locker shut. But truthfully, the person that is most upset about the grade is still *me*.

By Wednesday, I can take my mind off the grade. I've adopted a "what's done is done" thought process until the next grade comes out. Plus, the stress was giving me acne.

"Hey," Slater greets me when I take my seat. Somehow, he always gets to art before me.

"Hi."

"How has your day been?"

"Eh. I'm tired as usual. I could really take a nap right now. I don't know why they stopped the nap breaks for high schoolers. We need them way more than the elementary kids."

"Exactly. I could totally go for a nap right now." He laughs. "So, I found out that I'm free today and if you're free too, we can go face a fear?"

My eyes widen. I did not think that we would be facing our fears so soon, and I've never hung out with a guy alone before. But I suck it up, put on a brave smile. "Yeah, let's do it."

"Sounds good, we can go right after this class."

"Um, yeah."

Mrs. Katz is on another rant, but I can't comprehend a word of it. All I can do is fidget with my pencil.

I don't even realize that the bell has rung until Slater asks, "Ready to go?"

"Um, yeah, let's do it."

I wish it wasn't an ego boost walking down the school hallway with a cute guy by my side, but it totally is. I feel like a main character in a teen Netflix movie.

He stops his strides in front of a silver Tesla SUV.

My eyebrows raise. "This is your car?"

"Um, yes." He rubs his neck sheepishly.

Despite the all-white interior and him being a teenage boy, his car is freakishly clean. I'm too curious and nosy for my own good so I blurt out, "How is your car so clean?"

He blushes. "I'm kind of a neat freak."

"I love that about you." I slap my hand over my mouth and now it's my turn to blush.

"Thanks. Now are you done admiring my car?" He laughs as he places his hand behind my seat to reverse.

The close proximity of his hand makes my face turn even redder. "Never."

He returns a dimpled smile, and now I totally understand why people say that they can feel butterflies.

"Seriously, we're facing my fear first?" I frown, straining my neck to look at a very threatening poster of a person's head detaching while riding a rollercoaster. The longer I stare at the poster, the more nauseous I feel.

"I drove." He raises his arms in surrender.

Above us, a cart full of screaming people whizzes by, and I come to the realization that I do not want to be one of those people. "Can I change mine to be something other than roller coasters?"

"Hey, we want our project to be as authentic as possible," he jokes. "Besides, roller coasters are fun."

"The baby ones are fun. This park, however, is obviously catered towards the extreme thrill seekers." I narrow my eyes. "But you obviously knew that."

"You have no evidence." He fake gasps. "Besides, we're doing this for authenticity, remember?"

"That was an admission of guilt."

"Oops," he winks. "Now come on scaredy cat. Let's go."

Another wave of protests erupt from my lips, but Slater merely brushes them off with a smile. Before I know it, we're standing in front of a ticket booth and getting handed colored slips of paper.

When I finish reading the slip, the desire to throw up returns in full force. "Slater, this is a waiver."

"They're required to have a waiver by law. I mean even ziplines have waivers." Slater tries to reassure me. It doesn't work.

"Ziplines are also scary," I grimace, but I give in to signing the waiver. When I attempt to pay, Slater stops me.

"I got it. You didn't even want to come here so it's only right that I pay," he insists.

I shrug and put my card back. I mean it was good logic.

The ticket person hands us two red paper wristbands decorated with skulls around it, and waves disinterestedly. "Have fun."

"I definitely won't," I mutter under my breath and Slater snickers.

"So where to first?"

"The tiniest coaster."

"But that's boring," he protests, but he walks with me to search for small rides anyways.

Unfortunately, there aren't any because this is an amusement park catered to the most extreme of thrill seekers. Everywhere

I look, towering rides twist into the sky, their loops and spirals mocking my hesitation. I wander through the chaos, the screams of excited riders echoing around me, until I find a bench tucked away near a quieter corner. I sink into it with a sigh, the weight of defeat pressing down on me, Until I find a bench tucked away near a quieter corner. I sink into it with defeat.

"How about we go on the scariest ride here and then afterwards we can go make fun of other people being scared." He pauses. "And get overpriced amusement park ice cream."

"I like the way you think. But what if we skip the scary ride and experience second-hand fear from others?"

He looks at me. "You got this, Isla. If you feel too scared, we can back out, no problem, but who knows? You might begin to love roller coasters."

"There's no possible world where I could love roller coasters," I protest. However, when Slater offers his hand to pull me up, I accept. Then my mind processes that I'm holding Slater Wesbrook's freaking hand, and my traitor face blushes. His hand is larger than mine, warm but not sweaty, and so soft. The only con is that it lets go too soon.

Of course, Slater leads me to the scariest roller coaster in the park. Painted all red and equipped with multiple huge drops, my mouth begins to water as my nausea reappears. I mean, the ride is called Dare-Devil for goodness' sake!

"Can't we go on a smaller rollercoaster? I'm scared of those too," I ask once we're in the long line for the behemoth. I'm worried for the people who made these lines so long. They consciously chose to ride this death trap.

"Nope. We're facing that fear of yours and doing it right."

"I hope you know that this won't take away my fear of roller coasters."

"But it will get us a good grade on that art project," he jokes.

"Oh shush." I feel another eyeroll coming.

"Hey, no doubts."

"Nope, so many doubts." I shake my head. "Let's leave? My fears can be left unfaced."

He turns me towards him. "You got this. Seriously." But all I can think about is his hands on my arms.

And now I'm speechless. *Great.*

Thankfully, or not thankfully, we're next in line for the metal death trap. Slater notices my ever-present anxiety and repeats, "No doubts, okay?"

"No doubts." I give in, despite the fact that my heart is beating out of my chest and my mind is thinking of endless possibilities. *No doubts.* He takes my hand and squeezes it in an attempt to comfort me, but instead my heart races faster.

The attendant loads us into a two-person cart at the very front and the height *really* hits me. And of course, it starts with a very big drop. Fun.

I pull the restraint over my lap and triple check that it's secured. "Tell my parents I love them."

"I promise you'll have fun."

"That's a very difficult thing to promise Wesbrook." I glare.

He winks, and says nothing.

The attendant checks all of our seat restraints, and I hyperfocus on the tiny, but existent gap between my stomach and the restraint. The restraint could become loose half way through the ride and I could fall out and die! At least my parents could get some cash from suing the amusement park. But it wouldn't be a lot, because the park looks underfunded. I curse at Slater in my head for not taking us to a more well-funded theme park.

When I try to push the restraint down further, the roller coaster starts to move. My knuckles turn white from gripping the sides, but the roller coaster stops to let us stare at the drop. How thoughtful.

Suddenly, wind rushes across my face and my stomach drops as we speed down multiple stories. I can't even keep my eyes open because I'm *that* terrified. And when the others scream out of enjoyment, I scream out of pure fear.

"Fun, right?" Slater asks and I can tell he's smiling from the tone of his voice.

I open my eyes to glare at him. "How are you not terrified?" I shout.

"The adrenaline rush is fun," he shouts back. What the heck is he talking about? Being scared for your life is anything but fun.

"I love pineapple on pizza, I can't roll my tongue, and I used to sleepwalk," Slater shouts into the air.

"What?" It's all so random that I start to laugh.

"Weird facts about you, go!" It's super obvious that he's trying to distract me, but it's also super sweet.

"I *really* love mayo, like I'll have it on anything, I can't snap, and I can't whistle," I shout into the air.

Surprisingly, the distraction works, because I don't realize that we're going down another drop until halfway through. We continue with the weird fact game until the roller coaster comes to a stop.

And somehow, I make it out alive.

"Never again." I shake my head when the roller coaster finally brings us back to safety. "Seriously, never again," I repeat with a glare.

"It was fun." A big, dumb smile stretches his face.

I keep shaking my head. My hands are numb from clenching the seat restraint, and my head is still spinning.

"Hey, you survived and now you won't ever have to ride a roller coaster for a school project ever again."

"I guess."

"Now we can go get ice cream and make fun of people's screams," he cheers, and I can't help but laugh. The. Slater. Freaking. Effect.

CHAPTER 9

The first thing I do when I wake up is lift my shirt to a mirror. Then I turn to the side to inspect the curve of my stomach and suck it in to test what I would look like if I was skinny. After a few more repetitions, my hatred of myself increases.

Before I know it, I've added another step to my morning routine.

I hate that I have multiple problems that I can't define, so I keep telling myself that I'm okay until I believe it.

My parents are at the kitchen table, sipping their chrysanthemum tea in fine china cups. These past few days, it has been either silence or shouting between us so I'm bracing for both.

When I take my seat, my mom pushes a plate of omelet and orange slices towards me. It's my favorite breakfast food and she knows it.

"Eat," she orders, but I know what it really means. In a one-word command, she conveys that she forgives me.

My dad addresses me for the first time in weeks. "The stocks you like are growing." It's brisk and to the point, and it's not even a compliment, but I smile so wide that my face starts to hurt.

"Oh, I almost forgot, the chair in your room was broken so I fixed it," he says.

I don't think my parents have ever directly told me that they loved me. Instead, they grant me these little gestures.

"Thanks."

"Eat your food, it's getting cold," my mom nags, but all I hear is "I love you."

It's a feeling like no other – an incomparable joy.

And it makes all the pain they inflict worth it.

Mrs. Robins and her purple lipstick of the day lectures on symbolism in literature, but my eyes go elsewhere. And by else-where, I mean Slater.

While the rest of the popular group is talking and joking around with each other, Slater remains silent with his eyes on Mrs. Robins. He's fidgeting with the sleeve of his gray basketball sweatshirt and his cheeks are flushed. *Cute.* Subconsciously, I trace his perfect side profile, and analyze his slightly upturned nose slope.

Apparently, I've stared at him for too long because Raina leans over to whisper, "You like him, don't you? My ship is sailing."

But of course, freaking Brent overhears. "Isla, you have a crush on someone from the popular table?"

"Mind your own business, Brent." I glare. But I'm also slightly angry at Raina because every time she talks about my business, someone overhears, and before I know it, I'm the subject of class scrutiny.

"Well, if he likes Asians, he might like you," Brent so helpfully informs me.

"Why do you feel the need to say something racist every time you open your mouth?" I deadpan.

"Now, how was that racist?" he asks, repeatedly clicking his pen.

"If you don't know how that's racist, maybe you need to re-evaluate your perception of racism."

"Which one do you like? The elusive Tyler? The sporty Derek? Wait, I know. The new kid Slater?" Brent continues. "You know, I'm surprised he got in with the popular crowd so quickly. I've been trying for years."

I don't let any emotion pass through my face. If Brent figured out who I had a crush on, I think I'd die. "They don't let in losers." I smile mockingly.

"Dang, Isla! Why are you so moody today? Is it because you're on your period?"

"Oh my gosh, Brent. Shut up for once in your life," Raina finally chips in.

Surprisingly, Brent listens and doesn't say another word for the rest of the class. Thank goodness. Now I can go back to staring at Slater.

Some really pretty girl has a hand on his arm and I feel my eyes narrow minusculely. Even life is telling me to chill out. Guys like him don't go for girls like me.

Gosh, I wish I was pretty.

Mrs. Robins' angry white board Expo writing distracts me away from further self-deprecating thoughts. "I'm sorry to those who were actually paying attention." She looks at Slater.

"But since everyone else seems to be so chatty today, we're doing a pop analysis on the purpose of symbolism! You guys won't have any trouble because you are obviously all experts on this subject already," Mrs. Robins yells. Dang it, we have broken Mrs. Robins.

The whole class groans in unison.

"No complaining. This quiz is going to be a testament to your wonderful multi-tasking skills. I don't know many people who can both talk and listen simultaneously, but it seems like everyone here has that skill set." Her smile combined with the purple lipstick makes her look like the Cheshire Cat. "Now everyone get out their laptops and open your Google Classroom quiz."

I reluctantly grab my super old, never updated laptop from my backpack, and observe everyone else's new laptops from the corner of my eye. Out of embarrassment, I shield the back of my laptop with my arms.

A painful pinch jolts me, and I know exactly who the attacker is. "Aisha, this habit of pinching me has to stop."

"Sorry girl. You weren't paying attention to me." She pouts. I motion for her to continue. "Oops, I lost my train of thought. Oh, right yeah, what font should I use?"

"Times New Roman is a classic," Elise chirps from over Aisha's shoulder. She interrupted me for *this* question?

"But I want to do something memorable and cool." Aisha frowns.

"Syne Mono looks cool." I suppress my eye roll.

"But then Mrs. Sheffield is going to think that my paper is haunted," Aisha replies. *Oh, she's got to be kidding me.*

"She's not going to think that," I snap.

Aisha deliberates for a few minutes before eventually settling for Times New Roman.

I, on the other hand, start typing up my analysis. And by typing up my analysis, I mean typing up sentence fillers. Over and over again. The scary part is, I submit my paper without a care for the bad grade I'm definitely going to get.

I'm numb.

Despite me arguing that we could meet at the hospital since it is way closer to him, Slater shows up at my house to pick me up. Today, we're facing his fear.

Even with a gray sweatshirt and morning hair, this boy looks good. "Good morning." He hands me a caramel frappe. I can't believe he remembered my drink choice.

"My hero." I beam.

A comfortable silence washes over us, and my thoughts wander. Eventually, they settle on the reason for Slater's fear of hospitals. I consider asking him, but something tells me that's too invasive of a question. I really am too nosy for my own good.

"You can change the radio if you want."

"Cool." I hate that he gave me this choice. I make a mental pro and con list between choosing a song that I think he would like, or choosing a song that I would like. But I'm selfish to the core, and eventually decide on a Taylor Swift song. When I hear Slater humming along, my head whips towards him.

"I appreciate her songs."

My jaw drops. "What. Seriously? Every guy I know is so against her."

"I'm not like the other guys." He attempts to keep a straight face, but a laugh breaks out anyway as he shakes his head at himself.

"Oh, my gosh, stop." I giggle. "You're so quirky."

"I know. I'm so quirky and different, and not like the other guys." He continues the joke, winking at me. "But seriously, you have to give credit where credit is due. She's great at what she does."

"Yes! I love you for saying that." Then I backtrack. "Not love, love, but like you as a friend, um yeah. I'm just going to shut up now and maybe jump out of the car." *Gosh, I hate myself. This has happened twice.*

But then Slater gives a full belly laugh and my embarrassment flits away. He has this way of making you feel comfortable around him.

Unfortunately, comfort leaves as fast as it arrives, and I plummet back to reality with the halt of his car. My grades are declining, and the only way I can get a guy to hang out with me is if we're stuck in a project together. And somehow, I've managed to make everything about me. *Again.*

"Are you ready?" I bump my shoulder against his.

"As ready as I'll ever be," he tries to convince me, but it sounds more like he's trying to convince *himself.*

"Lead the way, Wesbrook."

He walks by my side and adjusts so that he is the one next to the road. After crossing many sidewalks and a car splashing water on us, Slater got the blunt of it, we arrive at the pediatric hospital. Inside, the hospital feels like a world apart from the city's noise. The air is cool and sterile, tinged with the scent of disinfectant. The walls are painted a soft, calming blue, adorned with colorful murals meant to ease the nerves of young patients.

When we approach the stone counter, a nurse calls out to him. "Slater Wesbrook, is that you?"

"Hi Linda." He waves.

"How is the family? Are they doing well?"

"They're doing good." His face is devoid of smiles, and his voice is dry. It's nothing like the Slater that I have grown to know.

"That's nice to hear, sugar. What are you doing here today?"

"I'd like to visit Room 323. It's for a school project."

"Yeah sugar, of course. You know where it is, right?" she asks, a trace of pity lining her voice.

"I don't think I can ever forget."

"Well, it was lovely to see you," Linda says. "I wish you best of luck on your project."

"Thanks."

Like every other hospital room, Room 323 has a single bed with machines next to it. The only difference is the collection of paintings pinned on the wall.

At the door, Slater takes a step back. "Yeah, I don't know if I can do this."

"Just being able to stand here makes you one of the bravest people I've ever known." I don't know what happened here, but the emotional scars it had left on him are obvious.

"Thanks Isla." He looks at me. "Seriously, thanks."

I smile. I like that I can be here for him like he was for me. "Of course. Do you need space to do this alone?"

"No. Your presence is the only thing that's giving me the strength to face it."

My ears ring, and my heart beats faster. I am absolutely touched.

He takes one more deep breath before stepping in. We stand in the room in silence for a few minutes until he speaks up. "This was my sister Willow's room."

"You don't ever have to explain anything to me." I whisper softly, putting a hand on his back to try to show my support.

"No, I want to. It's about time I talk about it with someone other than my parents and my therapist." he smiles in a self-depreciating way. "She died of brain cancer about three years ago. She was only nine."

I don't even notice I'm crying until I feel familiar warmth tears trickle down my face. "I'm so sorry." I wrap my arms around him, and he hugs me back. His shoulders are shaking.

"I couldn't deal with her death. I was spiraling and chasing thrills to make myself forget." His voice cracks. "That is the real reason why my parents transferred me to Alistair Cabot."

My heart breaks for this boy, and the only thing I can do is hug him tighter.

"Sometimes I wake up and expect to see her tugging my arm, begging me to watch a Barbie movie with her. But then I realize that she's not there and she'll never be there again." His tears are heart breaking. "I hate that I took all those moments for granted."

"You are so strong. You being willing to face all this for a stupid art project is a testament to your strength. Not everyone can go through a situation like that and still find the light in life. You should be proud of yourself."

"Thank you for everything." He looks at me, and now we're both sobbing messes.

When my eyes gravitate towards the paintings on the wall, Slater tell me, "She painted all of those and made her doctor swear that she would leave the paintings up for the next person."

He tugs my hand towards a painting of a castle in the clouds and angels guarding it. It's a child's perception of Heaven and acceptance of what was happening to her. I feel another wave of tears rising again.

"She was very talented." I choke on the words.

"Willow used to make Mom and Dad run to the art store weekly for paint." He grins in a way that only a proud sibling can, and my heart breaks all over again.

It's not fair.

CHAPTER 10

It's another freezing day at Beans. I wish I was happy here, drinking iced coffee and marinating in the presence of my friends, but then, what is happiness? It's just a made-up concept that we associate with endorphins.

Gosh, I'm really leaning into my teenage angst.

To distract myself, I focus my attention out the window. Snow is cascading, and it's sparkly and disastrously beautiful. Some snowflakes land on the window so I make stories for them. The biggest snowflake is Marsha, who is secretly in love with Dave, the snowflake closest to the edge, who is getting married to Julie, the perfect, tiny snowflake.

Aisha snaps her fingers. "Oh yeah, where's Naveen today, Raina?"

I'm reminded once again that all my friends have romance in their lives. Grades were supposed to be *my* thing, but now I have nothing.

"His name is Mark for the hundredth time, and he doesn't work today." Raina groans.

"That sucks." Aisha pouts. "We have to start coming when he's working. Maybe he'll give us a discount."

"What are you guys typing your essay on?" Elise asks.

"Feminism in Pride and Prejudice," Aisha boasts.

"Symbolism," Raina says.

"Gosh, Raina, you're such a suck up." Elise laughs.

"I want a good grade." She winks.

I shrug because I haven't even looked at the prompt. I hate myself for this, but I can't seem to do anything about it. It's like I'm a bystander to my own life. While they refocus their attention on their work, I scroll through social media.

"I feel like my reasoning isn't good enough." Elise frowns, tapping her finger against the table anxiously.

Raina peeks at Elise's laptop. "You can always add more details to support your opinion."

Elise takes a sip out of her medium sized pumpkin spice latte. "Raina, I literally don't understand what you just said to me. My mind is fried."

"It looks good, I promise," Aisha claims, which I find slightly suspicious because Aisha hasn't even glanced at Elise's laptop once.

Raina turns her attention onto me. "Isla, are you not working on your essay?"

"I'm not in the mood right now."

Everyone stops what they're doing to stare at me in concern.

"What? I'll do it at home." *I probably won't.*

"Wow, I never thought I would see the day that Isla Wu would decline an opportunity to finish her work early," Aisha snarks.

"Gosh, you make me sound like such a nerd." I roll my eyes jokingly. "I'm trying something different." *No, I'm not. I just don't have the motivation for anything.* Satisfied with my answer, they leave me alone, and change the topic.

I wish they didn't. I wish they would investigate further and help me, but we can't have everything we wish for, can we?

"How is Naveen anyway?" Elise asks.

"You guys are never going to accept that his name is Mark, right?" Raina asks, exasperated.

"Nope," Aisha states, enunciating the p sound.

Raina somehow continues typing as she talks. "He's doing good. I'm not as experienced with dating as you guys are so I have no idea how to do this whole thing. All I know is that I really enjoy being around him." Why couldn't she just say Elise and Aisha? I am obviously not included into this mix.

"Girl, I wish I had what you had with Naveen. You guys are so cute. My boyfriends have at most lasted for a month." Elise frowns.

"It's because you choose the worst guys, Elise," Aisha states.

"I guess you're right. The next one's going to be different though, I just know it." Elise winks at us. Dang, I almost forgot that Elise likes Slater. "Raina, do you have any tips for me?"

"I mean with Mark. He was the one who made the first move so I'm not the best person to ask."

Elise pouts. "Slater won't pay any attention to me."

"Babe, why are you so hung up on him anyways? So many people are just waiting in line to date you," Aisha reminds her.

"There's just something about Slater, Aish," Elise responds, and internally I agree.

As the conversation continues to revolve around dating, I become an outsider. Again. "Hey, guys, I think I'm going to head home. My parents are expecting me to be home by now," I lie through my teeth.

"So soon?" Elise frowns.

"Yeah, unfortunately."

"We miss you already." Aisha pouts.

I blow them a kiss. "Miss you too."

Outside is truly a winter wonderland. I just wish that I was in the mood to appreciate it more. I take a swing out of my caramel latte like it's alcohol, and maybe it's liquid courage from my non-alcoholic drink, in my defense, caffeine is a drug. But I take out my phone and text Slater.

Me: *Hey wyd?*

He texts back a minute later.

Slater: *Nothing. Want to do something?*

Me: *Yeah, maybe we can go face a fear.*

Of course, my reason is school related. I'm too big of a coward for anything else.

Slater: *Where should I pick you up?*

A smile begins to form on my face.

Me: *Just shared my address with you.*

Slater: *I'll be there in ten.*

True to his word, Slater does arrive in ten minutes. I've never been so happy to see his car.

"Hey you." He smiles when I get into the car.

"Hey. Should we go face a fear?" I ask.

"That's my Isla, always right down to business." He laughs. "Which one?"

I try to not freak out over the fact that he just indirectly called me his, and ponder for a bit before responding, "I mean I'm scared of driving."

"Do you have your permit?"

"Yeah."

"Okay, great. I'm scared to be driven around people who are scared of driving so two birds, one stone."

I playfully hit his arm. "Stop. That's not funny." But the corners of my mouth double-cross me.

"I'm absolutely serious." He keeps his straight face for a minute, before he starts to smile too.

Something had changed between us since the hospital. I don't know what, but it was *something*.

Slater types Coney Island into the GPS.

"The beach? Really?" I ask.

"The beach is the best place to learn anything."

"Isn't it snowing right now?"

"Even better." He winks.

Before I know it, Slater parks in front of a tiny Coney Island storefront boasting one-dollar pizzas. He opens my door and gestures for me to get into the driver's seat.

I stare at him, and I even try puppy eyes. "Do I have to?"

"Yes." He smiles cheekily. "Quickly, though. The parking is metered and I haven't paid, so, technically, we're breaking the law."

I roll my eyes. When I get into the driver's seat, my leg starts bouncing uncontrollably and my hands shake. "I cannot believe you're trusting me with your nice car right now."

"I trust you." He's so earnest.

Gosh, why does he have to do this? "Where am I supposed to drive?" I ask, pretending that his words don't affect me.

"Around." He smirks as he leans back with his arms behind his head.

"That's not helpful at all. Address please."

"Wherever your heart desires."

"Oh my gosh Slater." I laugh in exasperation.

"I'm serious. Wherever you want to go. *Mi carro es tu carro.*" He wiggles his eyebrows at me.

"The saying is *mi casa es tu casa*," I correct as I type in the address for an ice cream shop. Hey, something yummy should come out of this!

"The saying is whatever you want the saying to be. Now come on let's do this!" He cheers.

It's a combination of trying to impress him and actually wanting to face this fear that gets me to slowly reverse the car onto the road. My heartbeat pounds in my ears and my lungs don't breathe normally, but I'm doing it. *I'm driving!*

And after a few too many hard brakes and accidental speed ups, I feel that I am getting the hang of this driving thing.

"Look at you, you're a natural."

I can just tell that he has a smile on his face. I'm too scared to take my eyes off the road to check. "I'm going ten miles below the speed limit, and all these other cars are either tailing me or trying super hard to pass me," I deadpan.

"So? Who cares what others think?"

"I do." I laugh, but it's not funny. It's a sad truth. Of course, right when I say that, someone honks. What the heck did I do now?

"Sorry!" I whisper, but I know the person can't hear me.

"You didn't do anything wrong. That person is just a butt-hole. Some people shouldn't have a license."

I really, *really* like that he is angry for me.

Surprisingly, we make it to the ice cream shop in one piece. Slater claps, and I take a mini bow or whatever is allowed with a seat belt. Honestly, it's more like a nod. I glance out the window. Snow on the beach is such a lovely, but weird juxtaposition.

A small part of me feels guilty for being so close to Slater when Elise tells me that she likes him every chance she gets, but the selfish part of me wins. I'm too happy to care.

Entering the ice cream shop just adds to my happiness. The warmth instantly hits me, a stark contrast to the cold air and the sight of snowflakes drifting down onto the beach outside. Inside, the cozy, brightly lit space smells like sweet vanilla and waffle cones, with tubs of vibrant, colorful ice cream lined up behind the counter. There's just something so comforting about eating ice cream, even when it's freaking snowing outside. "Vanilla please," I tell the employee behind the counter. Slater orders chocolate.

Slater reaches into his pocket to get his debit card, but I beat him to the chase and stick my tongue out at him.

"Hey, I could've paid," he protests, pouting.

"You always pay. It's my turn to treat you to something." I wink at him and tap my ice cream to his. "Cheers."

The first lick is splendid, yummy, and everything that ice cream should be, but the second lick brings guilt, pain, and my mom's words. *Should I really be eating this?* I stare at my thighs. *Gosh, I'm already too fat.*

Slater's voice interrupts my thoughts. "Hey, look, the board-walk is right outside, and there's one game that isn't closed."

"That's slightly sketchy, but let's check it out."

It's an under-budgeted goblet toss game with scary off-brand stuffed animals as prizes. I mean there's a freaking stuffed animal named Furious Georgiana. With too much blush and black serial killer eyes, I understand why Furious Georgiana was kept a secret.

"You're kidding." I can't help but snort as I look through the other characters.

"This is why we are open during the off season. No one comes here during peak season. I'm not going to lie, working in this close proximity to them gives me nightmares sometimes." The girl behind the booth shivers. "Um, no, I take that back, they're great. Ugh, what am I kidding, I can't even lie to you guys. Please don't get me fired."

Slater and I both laugh. "We promise we won't get you fired," he says.

"Thanks. So, do you guys want to try your luck to win some weird stuffed animals?" she asks.

"Absolutely," I say. "The stuffed animals kind of remind me of myself." No one reacts to my comment so I start doubting my joke telling skills.

"Well, here you go." She dumps a handful of ping pong balls into our hands.

Unfortunately, I suck at boardwalk games. After seeing the balls bounce off the corners too many times, I start to squeeze my eyes shut after I throw. Mr. Perfect, on the other hand, sinks every ball he tossed into a goblet.

"Spent too much time here with my dad and Willow as a kid." I can't stop the smile that arises on my face when I picture a little Slater and Willow tugging their dad to every booth.

"Which weird stuffed animal?" the girl asks. Slater turns to me to ask the same question.

My eyes crinkle with excitement. I've never gotten a stuffed animal from the boardwalk before. Heck, I've never even played a boardwalk game before. My parents always said they were money scams. "Wait, really?"

"Absolutely. Choose." He waves toward the toys.

Of course I have to go with my girl Furious Georgiana. What can I say? She just spoke to my inner soul. "Thank you." I beam.

He smiles, "No problem."

I hear a few sniffles, and I turn to find the worker crying. "You guys are just too cute. It's like watching a movie play out in real life." She snatches multiple tissues from who knows where. "Sorry, my fiancé dumped me a week ago. Now I'm just a pathetic loser who operates a boardwalk game during winter." Then she shoots a warning glare at us. "Never break up you guys."

Neither of us had the heart to tell her that we weren't dating.

CHAPTER 11

"Love your body" is the heading of the lavender pamphlet on my lap. As if it's easy, like it's a switch that I can just flip. Like it's a freaking choice.

"I hate guest speakers," Raina mutters as she takes the seat beside me.

"Apparently the subject is body dysmorphia," Aisha chimes in.

"At least I secured us good seats with a view." Elise waves her arms in front of her like she's revealing a prize on a gameshow.

Raina rolls her eyes. "The view of the back of the popular guys' heads?"

"Goodness, Raina, if you want to see their faces so bad, all you had to do was ask." Elise smirks. "Connor, Brady, Slater, Elliot," Elise calls in the high-pitched voice she adopts around guys. I don't know whether to feel bad or happy for Robin, the other member of the group.

But, of course, the boys in front of us all turn around. Even Robin.

"How was your day?" Elise giggles, even though nothing is funny. Connor and Brady take this opportunity to launch into a long, oddly descriptive story.

"Good, Elise. Thank you for specifically asking me." Robin beams. When Elise ignores him again, I start to ugly laugh. Snorts, watery eyes, and all.

When everyone turns to look at me, my face heats up.

"What's so funny?" Elise asks.

"Oh, nothing," I say.

Most of them turn around, but one eye remains on me. "Hi, Isla," he grins.

"Hi." I wave back.

"Can I be let in on the secret?" he asks with puppy eyes.

I gesture for him to lean closer so I can whisper in his ear. "Elise ignoring Robin," I point at them. "Look!"

At the sight of Elise turning her head when Robin tries speak, we both start to cackle. My stomach hurts by the time I finish laughing.

Like a second sense, I feel Raina's smirk. "We're just friends, okay?" I mouth to her.

She only raises her eyebrows in a "whatever you say" kind of way.

But it's the truth. Maybe I do have a slight crush on him, but doesn't everyone? I mean, Elise is the prime example. Her eyes are solely on Slater, even with Connor and Brady vying for her attention. But I can't blame her, because only through boys does she find her value. It's messed up, but she's a product of her circumstances.

Elise never wants to talk about her parents but from what I know, their divorce destroyed her. Her mom never wants to see her, while her dad focuses on dating girls close to Elise's age instead of paying attention to his *own* daughter. The neglect is so bad that Elise practically lives on her own.

Boys are the only place where she can find the attention she craves.

Finally, a lady approaches the stage. She taps the microphone three times before speaking into it. The third time makes the microphone screech. "Hello, can you guys hear me?"

A bored chorus of "yes" echoes back at her.

"In case you haven't guessed, my speech for you guys today is about loving your body." She pulls up a PowerPoint with the phrase "Just Eat" in big, green letters. "So, first I want to say, just eat," she pauses, expecting laughter.

Instead, she gets silence.

The lady struggles with changing the slide for a good minute. "Sorry, guys." The controller wouldn't budge even when she furiously clicks it. "Technology, am I right?" She attempts another joke, but the only people laughing are her and a couple of teachers.

Her next slide is a chihuahua side by side with a chubby Newfoundland dog. "We don't judge dog breeds because of their size so why should we judge ourselves?"

When her next attempt to change the slide fails, she gives up. "Since time and technology seem to be against me today," she pauses in another attempt at comedic timing. *Gosh, sister really needs to chill out with the joke attempts.* "Um, well, the summary of my speech is you're beautiful, love your body, and just eat."

Pity claps fill the auditorium as everyone shoves their way out of the awkward atmosphere.

I leave hating my body even more. Unfortunately, I still have gym after the assembly.

As expected, Coach Crosby chooses two male athletes as captains.

A super tan freshman rolls her eyes. Since I'm trigger happy, I say to her. "He's such a misogynist."

"Yeah." When she turns to face me, recognition lights her face. "Hey, you're that girl who got knocked over by a dodgeball, aren't you?"

It looks like my reputation does precede me. "Yeah. The name is Isla." I laugh.

"Lindsay," she replies. "I felt second hand pain for you, but seeing that flustered look on Crosby's face was probably worth it."

"Yes, definitely worth it." I chuckle.

She laughs along with me. Looks like I finally met someone else in gym class. All it took was four months and a nose injury.

Sadly, my new acquaintance is athletic, which means she is one of the first called onto a team.

As usual, I'm the last one picked, but Slater is on my team which makes all the embarrassment worth it. He shoulder bumps me and greets me with his signature dimpled smile.

After gym, I trudge across the campus to get to the art building. The grass is sprinkled with students talking to their friends, scrolling through their phones, and even taking naps. It's freaking cold outside, but they don't care.

On the other hand, the art classroom is a juxtaposition of the lawn where blank, tired faces welcome me.

I look at Slater. "Everyone looks so gloomy."

"They're tired of Katz lectures."

"That's valid. How was your day today?" I ask.

Slater stifles his yawn. "Super boring, how about you?"

"The assembly was terrible, and capture the flag drained my soul."

"These freshmen are too competitive." He laughs. "It's capture the flag, not the end of the world."

I hold a finger over my lip, "Shhh, they don't know that." He laughs even harder. It's kind of an ego boost.

Mrs. Katz looks up from her phone to declare that we're working on projects today. I guess she must not have any problems today.

"Maybe it's going to be a good day after all," Slater whispers in my ear. Whispering is such an intimate action, like it's us against the world.

"What are our final fears?" I ask.

"Snakes." He grimaces.

"Oh my gosh, I have a fear of spiders!"

"Zoo trip?" He asks enthusiastically.

"Zoo trip." I confirm, my eyes fixated on his smile. Like a moth to a flame, I can't look away.

"You can't sit around all day," my mom says. "You know, even neighbor Mr. Zhou noticed your weight gain."

Just like that, I'm on the verge of crying. *Great.* "It's a Saturday, and Mr. Zhou is fifty years old. He has no right to comment on a teenage girl's body."

"You'd be pretty if you lost twenty pounds." She ignores my comment. I should expect this by now. After all, this is my perfectionist mom who demands perfection from me.

But I can never measure up.

Then I think about the body positivity speech, and I start to cry.

"Island, you're so fake. You wouldn't be so *pàng* if you weren't lazy. Are your grades getting better at least? You can't be both dumb and ugly." My mom is on fire today with these insults. Knowing her, she probably just had a fight with my dad.

I'm *always* a casualty.

I shrug. My grades aren't getting better, so I guess I am dumb *and* ugly. "Okay, Mama."

"You know, someone on WeChat's daughter got into Harvard, and she's skinny and pretty. Why can't you be more like her?"

That's when my last string of composure breaks. "Can you stop comparing me to other people? What if I started comparing you to other mothers? Look at Raina's mom. I know for a fact she doesn't call Raina fat all the time like you do to me."

"Don't talk back to me," she screams before slamming my door shut in her blaze of fury. Knowing my mom, she'll probably ignore me for the rest of the week, or at least until I beg for her attention and tell her that she was right and I was wrong.

And maybe she is right. The only thing I know is that long after she's gone, her words stay with me.

CHAPTER 12

It's that time of the year again. Sweaty palms, handmade posters, feigned surprise, crestfallen faces. If Alistair Cabot wasn't known for their academics, they'd be known for their lunchroom winter formal proposals.

Elise gets asked every year, of course. Raina, Aisha, and I have even made an event out of it, with chocolate mints and everything. It's like watching reality TV. Over the years, some boys have even run away from her, unable to handle the pressure.

"Did you remember the chocolate mints?" I elbow Aisha as we're in the line for greasy, square pizzas.

"Do I ever forget?" Aisha winks as she pulls the stash out from her backpack.

"You rock." I fist bump her. Aisha returns it with a little too much force and my knuckles hurt for a good minute after.

Armed with pizzas and my side of mayo, I'm weird, I know, we find Elise and Raina already eating at the lunch table.

"The line was long." I frown as I take my seat next to Raina.

"Is Mark taking you to the formal?" Aisha asks Raina.

"Yeah, I'm really excited." Raina smiles.

"How'd he ask?" Elise interrogates.

"It was super casual, I told him about the formal over Snap, and then he called me saying that he wanted to take me." Raina shrugs, acting nonchalant, but a ghost of a smile breaks her lips.

I squeal. That is the perfect proposal for the grand gesture hating Raina. It's so romantic that he knows her so well.

"Oh," Elise replies unenthusiastically. "That's," she pauses. "Nice."

The table goes silent. It's awkward and uncomfortable, and I hate it.

"Um, who do you think is asking you to the formal this year, Elise?" Aisha shifts the focus of the conversation.

"I'm not sure. You guys know who I want to ask me, but he still hasn't gotten the hint." Elise groans, staring straight at Slater.

I shouldn't be sad that Elise likes him because he doesn't like me like that, but I am.

"He doesn't like you," Raina mutters under her breath. I sigh in relief when Aisha and Elise don't react.

I love that Raina is always on my side, but sometimes I'm terrified she'll say something drastic and our fragile friend group will break apart.

Scuffing of shoes squeaks against the cafeteria floor and before long, Connor is at our table with a box of donuts.

"Aisha, get the mints." I kick her leg. Before I know it, I'm on my third chocolate mint, and Connor hasn't even started talking.

When Connor finally opens the box, showcasing the question "FORMAL?" in giant, sharpie letters, Elise just stares.

"Elise, say yes so we can get donuts." Aisha nudges her and whispers frantically.

"Did any of your other friends want to ask me?" Elise asks, making it obvious that she is looking at Slater. I feel bad for Connor. I would've automatically said yes if he asked *me*.

But boys didn't ask me to the formal.

"Um, no?" Connor shifts his weight, eyes darting back and forth from his lunch table to Elise. "Boy code," he jokes, chuckling awkwardly.

I grab another chocolate mint from the pack. I don't even know how many I've consumed. I stopped counting at seven. Aisha and Raina have the same idea, and our hands bump into each other.

"Sure," Elise gives him a smile that doesn't completely reach her eyes, and takes the box of donuts from him.

Connor fist pumps, and heads back to his lunch table. We hear a faint "She said yes!" and his friends cheering.

"Elise, that was kind of harsh." I wonder how she could be so rude.

"What, why? I just wanted to know if Slater was planning to ask before I accepted. Would you rather me accept, and then say no? I was doing it for him." Elise picks at her bright pink nails.

"You didn't have to do it so rudely. He spent money on that proposal," Raina backs me up. "He deserved a simple yes or no, without you asking him about his friend."

"Whatever. Not all of us can get excited over simple stuff like you do. If someone I was dating had asked me to the formal over freaking text, I would dump him so quickly." Elise gets up from her chair. "Besides, he was really happy, I mean we all heard him. Instead of reprimanding me, maybe you should be praising me for agreeing to go to winter formal with a guy I don't even like," Elise storms off.

"He called me and asked, which you would've known if you paid attention to anyone other than yourself," Raina calls after her.

Aisha grimaces, grabs a strawberry donut, and runs after Elise.

This is exactly what I was afraid of, and it was all *my* fault.

Thankfully, by Friday, Raina and Elise have forgiven each other. Talk between them, however, is still uncomfortable. I wish I didn't press the subject before, but what's done is done.

Alas, after a whole week of cute proposals and frenzy over outfits, the winter formal encroaches upon us. It's all anyone can talk about, and third period AP US History is just another testament to this.

"Who's taking you to the formal?" Lucy asks Elise over my shoulder.

"Connor, how about you?" Elise replies.

"Oh, my goodness, I'm going with Brady. We're going to be bumping into each other a lot! I wonder if Brady and Connor will rope us into a group dance." Lucy sighs dreamily. Her tone changes unkindly when she turns to me. "What about you, Isla?"

"I'm going by myself." My cheeks get hot. It's what I was expecting, but I'm still kind of bummed.

The only guy that texted me this week asked me about math homework. Like I'm the person to ask about math anyways, I freaking failed a test and my grade has been free falling since.

"Oh. Maybe you'll have better luck next year," Lucy says. "I don't think I've ever gone to the formal without a date. I think it's so embarrassing to go alone. You're so brave, Isla."

It's official, I hate Lucy.

"Connor told me that so many girls turned Brady down. Thank goodness he finally found someone desperate enough to say yes," Elise's voice is saccharine sweet.

I beam. The thing that I love most about Elise is that she will never hesitate to stand up for you.

Lucy doesn't say another word after.

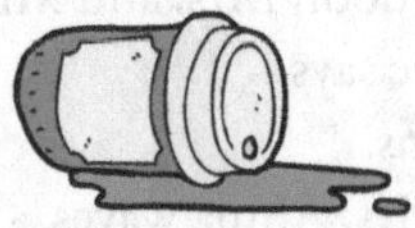

Finally, winter formal day arrives in all its glory.

Lying in my sparkly silver dress on Raina's rug, I feel kind of like a disco ball. Eventually, I get bored of waiting on my friends to get ready. "Raina, where's your mom's ABH eyeshadow collection?"

"Over here," Raina gestures at the beige-colored cabinets next to her.

I reluctantly get up from the rug to grab the eyeshadow. "Thanks!"

"Isla, babe, your hair is all messy now," Elise frowns, beckoning me over to the seat next to her. "Come here."

While I do my eyeshadow, Elise fixes my hair. I'm made too aware of my mono-lids as I try to follow a YouTube eyeshadow tutorial. My end result is nothing like the person in the video's, so I scrub the eyeshadow away with a makeup wipe. It makes my eyes burn, but I'd rather be in pain than look like a clown.

When we're all finished getting ready, we line up to look at ourselves in Raina's full-length mirror. I spin in my high heels, and smile faintly at myself. I feel kind of pretty for once.

Elise forces us to finish our pajamas to dress transformation on TikTok before we leave. It will probably go viral, and the comment section will be full of people commenting on how pretty they are, and how self-conscious I must feel around them.

I mean, it's already happened once.

"Ready to go?" Aisha asks. The hot pink stilettos increase the already present height disparity between us, and I have to strain my neck to look at her.

"Yes." We cheer.

Before we open the door, Mrs. and Mr. Ahuja catch us. "No drinking, no drugs," he says.

"Papa," Raina groans.

"Have fun, girls." Mrs. Ahuja waves.

"Love you, second parents," Aisha calls out, and everyone laughs. Sometimes I wish I had Aisha's conversational skills. Instead, I make people feel uncomfortable around me.

When we get into her car, Aisha taps the steering wheel and asks, "Hey Betty, sweetie, are you ready to go?"

"You are not talking to your car right now," Raina snorts.

"Betty only operates when given love and affection," Aisha says.

"Betty is a new BMW," Raina shoots back. "She will operate no matter what."

Aisha covers the sides of the steering wheel. "Not in front of her, she's sensitive about her age. Betty likes to think of herself as an old soul."

"Oh, my gosh, Aisha." Elise chuckles as she pats Aisha's seat in front of her. "Put on some music and drive already."

"Yes, ma'am. You better give me a five-star rating *and* a tip." Aisha twists her body to salute Elise before punching the radio button.

I stare out the window, and watch skyscrapers whizz by. The starless night combined with Aisha's over the speed limit driving makes the buildings blend into each other, creating kaleidoscopes of black and white light.

I'm kind of sad when we arrive at the five-star hotel venue. I wish I could be in the car, thoughtlessly admiring the beauty of the night longer. Instead, I'm headed straight towards my version of teenage hell. School dances.

Elise steps out of the car first. In her floor length white dress and red lipstick, she looks like a movie star going to her hit movie premiere. "Come on guys!"

While Raina and I walk towards the entrance together, Aisha stays behind to hand her keys to the valet. I instantly regret not bringing a jacket when the cold December wind brushes against my arms.

Elise checks our names in with the receptionist, who points us towards the elevator, and tells us to get off at the sixty fourth floor.

On the elevator, two elderly women ask us why we're dressed so fancy, and leave us with peppermints so that "your dates won't leave you because you have bad breath." I consider telling them that I don't have a date, but I refrain. I've reached my bitterness limit for the week.

The elevator flashes a red sixty-four, and announces our arrival with a ding.

Synthetic snowfall, chandeliers, marble floors, white tables, and floor to ceiling windows greet us. My head spins when I look through the window. It's *too* high and all I can think about is how I will fall to my death if the window breaks. Just in case, I move away. Hey, you never know what's going to happen.

Black and white uniformed caterers dot the place, lugging around platters of Hors d'oeuvres. Alistair Cabot really outdid itself.

"Elise, there you are." Connor pops out of nowhere to slip a rose corsage onto Elise's wrist. "You look beautiful, as usual."

Brady and Lucy stand beside him with smiles on their faces.

"Lucy, where did you get your dress?" Elise asks, looking her up and down.

Lucy's smile grows wider. "Saks."

"So, that's where I remember it from." Elise turns to us and says loudly, "I saw this dress on a mannequin, and I felt bad for the poor, tasteless soul who would choose to wear it. You're so brave, Lucy."

It's terrible, but I can't help but feel special that Elise is holding this grudge for *me*.

Brady steps away from Lucy like she's got some contagious disease, and Lucy's face flushes as she wraps her arms around herself.

"Connor, want to dance?" Elise holds her hand out nonchalantly.

"Of course." Connor takes her hand and they make their way to the dance floor. Despite Elise humiliating her, Lucy, and Brady scamper behind them.

Mark pushes through a crowd of people to get to Raina. It's a scene straight out of a movie. In his slim burgundy tie, he matches Raina's dress.

"Raina, you are breathtaking," Mark twirls her around.

I beam and make a heart with my hands. It seems that our roles have been reversed because now it's Raina who rolls her eyes at me as she leaves with Mark.

"Well, I guess it's just us." I turn to Aisha, but she's looking around the room for someone. She finds the person and also heads off. I have a good feeling that it's Isaac.

"Well, I guess it's only me." I sigh. Everyone else is out on the dance floor, so I take a seat at one of the white cloth-covered tables in the middle of the venue. I know for a fact that I look lonely, but I'm too mentally exhausted to care.

Besides, a slow song is playing, so even if I wanted to go to the dance floor, I couldn't.

I empty the sadness with hors d'oeuvres. Food is always there for me, unlike everyone else in my life.

"Looks like someone's having fun," a voice behind me announces. I know exactly who it is because who else sneaks up on me?

"What else is a girl to do?" I smile weakly, turning my attention back to scoffing down finger foods.

"Your friends left you too, huh?"

"Yeah."

He takes a seat beside me, and we fall into comfortable silence. I think silence is only comfortable around him. Out of the corner of my eye, I admire him. With his black tux and sparkling, thunderstorm eyes, Slater looks as handsome as ever.

"Why didn't you ask someone to the formal? You know anyone would've said yes if you asked," I blurt out. "Now you have to sit over here with lonely, loser me."

"What if I told you that I enjoy sitting over here with you and that I wasn't sure if the girl I wanted to ask would say yes?" He grins cheekily as he steals one of my cheese tarts.

I glare at his hand. "I'd say you're weird and a liar. Even I didn't choose to spend one of my last winter formals like this. Besides, who wouldn't want you as a date? You're like the ultimate catch," I inform him with a mouth full of buffalo chicken bite.

"The ultimate catch, huh? I'll keep that in mind for the next time I want to ask this girl to a dance."

I roll my eyes, but I would be lying if I said I wasn't jealous. Whoever caught Slater's attention does not even begin to understand how lucky she is.

"Don't let it get to your head."

"I'll try not to." Slater smirks. "Now, will you prove your own theory correct and say yes to me asking you to dance?" He bows, dramatically offering his hand.

"You're such a dork." I laugh, but I take his hand and let him guide me to the dance floor anyway.

A slow song is playing in the background, his hand is on my waist, and I can't think about anything except the fact that I am dancing with Slater *freaking* Wesbrook. I realize now that I don't mind if he never likes me back, just knowing him is *enough*.

"Are the social recluses really dancing in public?" He jokes.

"You're anything but a social recluse." I laugh. "Me on the other hand..."

Slater fakes an angry look. "Are you seriously kicking me out of the loner club that we formed together?"

"Fine, you can be an honorary member."

He ponders for a minute. "I deserve more, but whatever. I'll take it only because I like you."

I pretend his words don't affect me, but my heart races. "Wesbrook, this is the first compliment you've ever given me."

"Is it really, Wu?" He pauses. "Well, I guess I have to step up my compliment game from now on."

Before I can respond, Elise stomps over to us with a betrayed look on her face, and all happiness evacuates.

Well crap.

"Hi, Slater." Elise sounds happy, but her smile is twitching and her face is so red that I can see it under purple spotlights. "Isla, can I talk to you?"

I shrug and let Elise lead me a few steps away from Slater. He's definitely still in hearing proximity so I don't understand why Elise guided me here.

"How could you? I like him, you know that," she whispers angrily.

"You're blowing this out of proportion. I promise you he doesn't like me that. We are just friends."

There's a misleading silence that makes me think everything is okay, but then Elise erupts again. "You shouldn't have agreed to dance with him."

Now I'm the one with the flushed face. "So, you'd rather I just sit there miserably as you guys have the time of your life?"

"Yes."

I sigh in exasperation. "You're being over dramatic. I wouldn't chase after him when I know that you like him. Besides, even if I did, he wouldn't like me back."

"You're right. I mean even your parents don't find you pretty," she responds so quickly. It's like she had the words armed and ready, just waiting for the day that she could finally fire them.

I gasp, and I can't stop my tears from flowing. All I *can* do is *feel*. The thing that hurts the most is that what she says is true. I just never thought Elise would use my insecurities against me. To think that I even felt beautiful tonight.

Silly, delusional, little me.

"Thanks for letting me know how you truly feel about me," I manage to choke out, my voice hoarse and my breathing rapid.

Elise covers her mouth with her hands and regret floods her face, wave after wave. "I'm so sorry, I didn't mean to say that."

"You might not have meant to say it out loud, but it's obviously what you were thinking." My tears continue to cascade until my face is covered in salty remnants and now Elise is crying too.

"You know that I didn't mean it. I'm sorry, I said it out of anger." She sobs.

When I turn to go, Elise grabs my arm. "Please don't leave."

I look at her for a brief moment before pulling away. Then I tear off the stupid heels that have been killing my feet all night and run towards the elevator. My vision is a blur, and all I know is that I have to get out of here. It's a shock that I don't run into anyone.

"Isla, wait," Slater calls after me. I reluctantly hold the steel elevator door open for him.

"You heard that, didn't you?" I ask, rubbing my cheeks. I can feel the mascara and tears mixture drying against my skin.

He nods, embarrassed, as he presses the button for the ground floor.

"Why would she say that?" I croak.

It's a rhetorical question for myself, but Slater answers anyway. "I don't know but she's wrong. You look beautiful tonight." He pulls me into a hug. "You *always* look beautiful."

"You're lying." I sob.

"I promise you I'm not. You're gorgeous, Isla. Inside *and* out."

"What are you even talking about? I'm jealous, judgmental, and bitter. If you haven't noticed, I'm kind of an awful person," I laugh self-deprecatingly.

He brings a finger under my chin, lifts my face, and I swear that I drown in his eyes. "I've known you only for a few months, but you've become the first person I search for in a crowded room. You have the biggest heart, you genuinely care about other people, and you're my favorite person to be around. I'm *captivated* by you."

"You're corny." My face flushes. This is, quite possibly, the nicest thing anyone has ever said to me. To distract myself, I wipe my tears away and get ink mascara smears on the back of my hand.

He chuckles and wraps an arm around me as the elevator dings. "Let's go. I'll take you home."

"Are you sure? You'll be missing the rest of the formal?"

"The formal was getting boring, anyway. You were the most interesting person there." He grins boyishly, the type of grin that only he can pull of, as we make our way through the hotel lobby.

I know I look like a mess with smeared makeup and bare feet, but I don't care. He is next to me and he just said he was captivated by *me*.

"Your friends probably won't enjoy hearing that." I joke through my tears. Just like that, I don't feel like crap anymore. He's got to be magic or something.

"They can get over it." He hands the valet his car ticket.

The cold breeze smothers me and I cross my arms and shiver. Again, regret circles through me as my mom's pitchy "bring a jacket, you're gonna get cold" speech reverberates in my head. While staring off into space, replaying today's events in my head, a warm fabric encloses around my shoulders. I look up and find that Slater has wrapped his navy suit jacket around me.

"Thanks." Butterflies flutter relentlessly in my stomach and I feel like the freaking main character for once.

He smiles in response. "I don't want you to get a cold."

I open my mouth only to close it a second later. I don't even know what to say.

"Wait, aren't you cold? It's like freaking twenty degrees out here." My thoughts come back to me. "I feel bad now. You shouldn't have to suffer for my stupidity." I begin to slip off the jacket, but he puts a hand on my back to stop me and my focus dissipates again.

"Don't worry about it. I'm fine." He holds my gaze.

I could've sworn our faces were moving towards each other before his car's blinding headlights interrupted us. *Dang it, car. Why couldn't you wait a few more minutes?* While the wind blows harder, I pull Slater's jacket closer to me. It's warm, comforting, and smells like him. I start to dread when I have to give it back.

Slater tips the valet, I type my address into his GPS, and then we are off, zooming through the dark. If he wanted to distract me from the horrible events of tonight, he succeeded. I close my eyes and focus on my breathing. *In, out. Inhale, exhale.*

When I open my eyes, I see my house, and realization hits. I fell asleep in his car, and we must have been here for a while because Slater is playing games on his phone.

"Hey, you're awake," he remarks. "Welcome back to reality. I bet it isn't as awesome as dream world."

"How long have we been in my driveway?" I ask groggily, rubbing my eyes and slipping off his suit jacket.

"About thirty minutes." He must notice my panicked expression because he quickly adds, "It's no big deal. My parents don't expect me home until eleven."

"Thank you so much. Like seriously. This is one of the kindest things anyone has ever done for me." No one has ever run after me to make sure that I was okay until him.

He looks at me and smiles. "Of course, Isla. Anytime."

As I open the car door and start to get out, he speaks so low that I think I imagine it. "You were the person I wanted to ask."

CHAPTER 13

Two weeks have passed by and Elise and I still haven't spoken to each other. When I see her walk towards me, I smile and speed walk in the other direction. Call me petty and unforgiving, but it still *hurts*.

After a few more days of strategized avoidance, Elise gets the memo. When we see each other now, nod, quickly avert eye contact, and go our own ways. It's kind of insane how quickly you can go from best friends to strangers.

At lunch, Raina and I sit next to each other at our usual table, but Elise and Aisha have moved.

"This is so weird." Raina pointedly moves her eyes to where Elise and Aisha are sitting. It's the popular girl table with Lucy and *those* types of girls, and it's right next to the popular guy table. I'd be lying if I said that it didn't hurt.

"I know," I say. "They didn't have to move."

"I mean, at least we're drama-less for once," Raina jokes. When she notices my grimace, she asks, "Too soon?"

"A little bit. I wish I could just get over it and forgive her, but I can't and I don't know why." I sigh.

Raina squeezes my shoulder. "She literally called you ugly, and we all know that you have some *serious* self-esteem problems."

"Raina!" I glare.

She raises her arms in surrender. "Hey it's true. I mean it doesn't make sense that you're as insecure as you are." Her words aren't much comfort.

"You don't have to lie to me, you know. I know I'm ugly, the people at this school know I'm ugly, and in general, the whole world knows I'm ugly." I shrug. "It may hurt, but I've accepted it." Which is one of the biggest lies I've told tonight. I hate myself.

"Isla, you know that's not true. You're so freaking hot," she says.

"Raina, I've witnessed the evidence." I keep the words emotionless. "Have you never noticed that whenever we go out, it's always people asking you guys out but not me?"

"Um no. You're totally wrong. Remember the curly haired guy with a skull T-Shirt at the mall?"

"He asked all of us out and was staring at Elise the whole time." I shake my head. "Besides, I'm pretty sure he just wanted to brag to his other freshman friends that he had more than one girlfriend."

"Okay then how about Ronny from that really hippy clothing store?"

"Raina, that's his job. He has to flirt with potential customers to gain a commission."

"Okay fine. Oh my gosh, Slater." She's looking behind me.

"He sees me as a friend and only called me pretty to stop my crying."

"You are such a glass half-empty person," Raina rolls her eyes. "But seriously look behind you. Wait, no don't." She looks at me and winks. "And you said you were just friends."

"We are," I insist.

To my shock, Slater arrives at our lunch table and takes a seat next to *me*.

"What are you doing here?" I ask.

"Having lunch like everyone else does during lunch time." He shrugs.

"Know-it-all." I playfully punch his shoulder and he only laughs in response.

Elliot calls out, "Wesbrook, you are a simp!" Slater responds with a playful wink. My face flushes with the implication, but once I notice that Elise is staring too, guilt overtakes the excitement.

Slater breaks the tension with his easy conversation and charismatic jokes. Raina's eyes dart back and forth between us, mouthing an "OMG" to me every time she thinks Slater isn't looking. He definitely notices, though, because a smirk remains on his face the entire time.

When lunch is over, Slater and I walk together to his car. Since we both have a free period last, we decide to go face our final fear...the zoo trip.

My phone buzzes with notifications from Raina, but I ignore them. She was definitely texting me to gush about Slater.

"So, why did you decide to sit with us at lunch today," I question him.

"Because I wanted to."

"But why now?"

"Maybe I finally gathered up the nerve to." He shrugs and giddiness flutters through me.

I poke his arm. "Scaredy cat."

He playfully raises both his hands in defense. "I guess I am. We can count that towards one of my fears."

"Stop trying to cheat your way out of facing fears." I roll my eyes.

He leans in so close that I can smell his minty breath. "Make me."

Usually I'd blush and look away, but this time, I stare right back. "Maybe I will."

Slater smiles and by the time we reach the car, we've bumped hands so many times that it can't be considered an accident anymore.

Halfway through the car ride, Slater groans, "Shoot, I forgot my wallet." He turns to me and asks, "Do you mind if we stop by my house real quick?"

"That's fine." I try to conceal my excitement. I'd be lying if I said that I wasn't curious to see what his house looked like. I'm nosy, I can't help it!

The silence falls again, but I choose to disrupt it. "I'll never understand how you like driving so much."

His eyes remain focused on the road. "It's kind of fun. Driving gives me this false sense of control." He sighs. "I'm never in control of the things that happen in my life."

It hits me once again that I'm not the only one who is struggling. I hate that I'm this self-centered. "Valid," I say awkwardly.

Slaters drives into the garage attached to a large cream-colored townhouse and parks in the empty space between two other fancy cars. I plan on staying in his car, but then he opens the door for me and holds his hand out. "My parents will get mad if I tell them that I left a girl waiting in my car." He sheepishly rubs his neck. *Gosh, he looks so freaking cute.*

Beaming, I take his hand and let him help me out.

Pictures and windows facing Central Park line the walls of the large staircase leading into the house. My eyes linger on a chubby-faced toddler Slater in a basketball uniform.

When we finish our ascent, a high ceiling and crystal chandelier galore awaits us. To the left, a hallway filled with flowers and paintings extends from the foyer. It's the type of house you'd find in *Architectural Digest*. Most of my friends are wealthy so I should be used to it by now, but that doesn't stop my mouth from dropping.

"Your house is stunning."

"Thank you, I designed it," a female voice pops up behind me. I turn around to find a beautiful, tall, blonde woman. Smartly dressed in a trench coat, black trousers, and red-bottomed heels, she embodies the word 'classy'. I want to be her when I grow up. It all clicks in my head. No wonder Slater is so handsome.

"Hey, Mom."

"Don't *hey mom* me. Introduce me to your lovely friend."

"Mom, this is Isla," Slater says.

"Nice to meet you Isla." Her smile is warm, and she has his thunderstorm eyes. Well, I guess technically he has *her* thunderstorm eyes.

"Nice to meet you too, Mrs. Wesbrook." I smile back, still in some kind of daze. Crap, what if she isn't married and her last name isn't Wesbrook! An apology makes its way onto the tip of my tongue.

She stops my incoming verbal vomit with an even bigger smile. "Please call me Jen. It's so wonderful to meet you." She looks behind her and calls out, "William, come here. Slater has finally brought a girl home!"

My cheeks instantly flush red. From the corner of my eye, I can see Slater blushing too. "Mom, please stop being so embarrassing."

"Oh, shush, this is a monumental moment." Jen grabs her phone and points it at us. "Slater, put your arm around her!"

"Mom." Slater groans, sliding a hand through his hair.

"Don't *mom* me. This will go on the wall. Now smile."

Slater stops his objections and wraps an arm around me.

"Is this a bad time to tell her that we're not a couple," I tippy toe to whisper into his ear.

"You don't want to deal with her matchmaking. If we tell her we're not a couple now, she'll do all sorts of things to ensure that we will be," he leans down to whisper back. I detect a tremor of fear in his voice which makes me laugh.

That's when the flash goes off. "Perfect." Jen beams. "There you are William. Come meet Isla!"

A tall man with peppered hair and a perfectly tailored suit heads towards us. How are they all so beautiful? They look like one of those families you'd find in magazines.

"Nice to meet you, Isla." He smiles, reaching out for a handshake. It's a firm handshake, the type that takes years in the corporate world to perfect.

"It's nice to meet you as well, Mr. Wesbrook."

"Please call me William. Welcome to the family. All I ask is just no overt PDA in front of us please, we have old people's eyes."

My jaw drops.

"Dad, you're not funny." Slater's face is getting redder by the minute. "Please never talk again."

William erupts into laughter. "Then how will I tell my jokes?"

Jen smiles at them before turning to me. "Now, Isla, dear, you must stay for dinner."

"We can't, we have to face a fear for our art project," Slater answers for me.

"Well, you must stay for dinner soon. I'll have Slater send out a message." Jen seems serious.

"Mom, we have to grab something," Slater takes my hand and guides me to the staircase.

On the walk up the stairs, Slater says, "I'm sorry about that. My parents are total weirdos."

The fact that his face is still red is adorable. I have this sudden urge to pinch his cheeks. "Don't worry, I found it endearing. They're awesome." I smile. A tiny bit of me can't help but compare his parents to my own.

"Don't let them hear you say that. Their egos will become even bigger and they'll quote you every time we argue." The urgency in his voice makes me laugh. "I'm serious." His protest only makes me laugh harder.

We pass another art-filled hallway to get to Slater's room. When he twists the black steel handle, I remark, "You must walk a lot each day."

"It's definitely an exercise. It sucks when you're in a bad mood, though."

"You're telling me the artwork doesn't lighten your mood?"

"Not when you pass them every day. Sometimes I get dreams where I'm transplanted into one of those paintings."

"That sounds like a good dream to have."

Slater shakes his head. "I've gotten better at handling them over the years, but eight-year-old me used to run to my parents' room and cry."

"Are you sure you don't do that anymore?" I joke.

"Maybe," he jokes back, looking straight at me. "You must take this secret to the grave."

"Pinky swear." I wink.

He laughs while pushing his door open. "Well, this is it."

Navy blue and white-themed, it's oddly neat for a teenage boy. A bathroom and walk-in closet extend from the room, and a basketball net hangs on his door. On one side of his wall are shelved basketballs and medals, while the other side consists of a giant computer, a bean bag chair, and a bookshelf, filled to the brim with books. Out of sheer nosiness, I walk over and inspect the spines of the books.

"Wait, you've read *Jane Eyre*?" I ask.

"I got bored, stole it from my mom, and never returned it." He searches through his cabinets.

"Stop. You did not!"

"I totally did. Finishing it gave me a superiority complex. I surprisingly enjoyed it."

"No wonder Mrs. Robins loves you." I giggle.

"Hey, I'm not ashamed. Jane was a total girl boss."

"Yeah, she was! I hate that she ran back to him in the end, though. I just hate Rochester. Dude was a walking red flag." My words make him laugh. "My only regret was not having an actual copy of the book."

He nods in response, and his eyes glance out the window for a second before returning to his search. After more rummaging, Slater calls out, "Okay, I found my wallet! Ready to go?"

Once we're in the car he turns to me. "Okay, hear me out. I know we planned to go to the zoo but what if we go to the aquarium instead because it's air conditioned and less smelly?"

"I'm down, but I don't think I'm scared of anything at the aquarium."

"We can make up something." He winks. "Sharks are scary, right? We can say we're both scared of sharks."

"Okay, sure." I concede with a snort. "This is a big change from the old you who wanted to ensure the authenticity of the project."

"Yeah, about that...I only said that so you would ride a roller coaster with me. Besides, we're in the home stretch now." My head is spinning. *He wanted to ride a rollercoaster with me! Stay calm, Isla!*

"That is so wrong. I will forever remember this deceit, Wesbrook," I tease, thanking God that I said something semi-normal.

"Oops." He doesn't sound the least bit sorry.

There's a moment of silence before I gather up the nerve to speak. "Thanks for what you did for me at the formal. I really do appreciate it."

"Of course, if you ever need a ride or someone to talk to, just call me." He takes his eyes off the road to look at me for a second. "I'm here for you."

"I feel bad that you always have to drive all the way to Queens. I'm such an inconvenience, but you're too nice to say anything."

"Trust me, you're the opposite of an inconvenience." He reaches out to squeeze my hand. I squeeze his hand back, but I don't believe him. All signs point to the obvious truth.

I try to stop talking, but my feelings have been bottled for so long that even the slightest crack will unleash the whole monster. "You know, I'm so tired of feeling sad and useless all the freaking time. It sucks." I pity laugh. "And I'm totally worried about applying to college. I don't have anything special about me which would get me into the elite college that my parents have been forcing on me since third freaking grade. I'm going to be mediocre forever! I mean, I was good at getting good grades until I wasn't. Now I'm failing all of my classes and my parents don't know, and I'm not pretty enough to rely on my looks for a living."

"I'm a big, freaking failure. What am I going to do?" I start to hyperventilate. My head spins, my chest hurts, and my throat constricts. I try to suck in air, but it's a failed effort.

Oh my gosh.

What is happening to me?

Why can't I breathe?

"Isla, you're okay, I'm here."

Focusing on his voice calms my fear, and Slater offers his hand for me to hold and it's then that I realize we are parked.

"You're having a panic attack, but it will pass. Try to breathe with me if you can."

He takes deep breaths in and out, and I try to follow his rhythm. After a few synchronized breaths, my head clears up and I can finally breathe normally. It's as if a blanket has covered me with peace and alertness. With the alertness, however, comes the embarrassment.

"I'm so sorry," I whisper.

"You did nothing wrong." He hugs me and lays his chin on the top of my head. "I'm happy you're okay."

I kind of hate myself, but I like him. "Thank you."

"And I don't know who made you feel that way, but they are wrong. There is nothing mediocre about you. Nothing. You're beautiful, special, smart, accomplished, and anyone who can't see that is blind or–"

I throw my arms around his neck and press my lips against his. It's one of those brainless actions that feel like an inevitable course of life.

When my brain starts working again, every thought tells me that I'm reckless and stupid, that he doesn't even like me like that, that I should pull away before I make things even more awkward, but then he kisses me back. My brain crashes again and all I can focus on is him and his minty lips.

He pulls back for a minute and asks, "Are you sure?"

"Yeah." We go back to kissing.

I'm free-falling into the abyss that is Slater Wesbrook and for once, I welcome the fall. Scratch that, I embrace the fall. If you told me a year ago that I'd have my first kiss outside a gas station, I'd laugh and shake my head but here we are.

When we pull apart for air, we look into each other's eyes and giggle.

"Well, that's that," I say.

It's not even funny, but in the spur of the moment it's the funniest thing ever. I laugh my stomach hurting, ugly laugh, and Slater is bent over dying of laughter.

"So, aquarium now?" I ask when the laughter ceases. Kissing doesn't change the fact that we're still awkward teenagers.

"Yeah." He smiles. It's the type of smile that lights up his entire face and reaches his eyes which makes me smile in return.

During that car ride, at the aquarium, and even when I tuck myself into bed that night, I can't stop smiling.

CHAPTER 14

It's rare when I get to see the sun rise. In fact, it's kind of an accomplishment.

I woke up before my alarm even went off, and didn't lay in bed for the hour after. Instead, I'm here, getting hypnotized by the watercolor sky. When I'm finally able to pull my eyes away, I text Raina.

Me: *I kissed him.*

Three gray dots flicker on and off the screen before Raina decides to facetimes me.

"Why am I only hearing about this now?" she squeals when I accept her call. To protect my hearing, I turn the volume down to the lowest level. "Where, when, what, how?"

"It just happened." I don't want to admit that my first kiss happened with my first panic attack.

She looks at me pointedly and I just shrug in response. "Well, I am so excited for you! My ship is sailing!"

I smile. I'd be lying if I said that it wasn't nice being the center of attention for once. "Enough about me, let's talk about you and Mark."

"Mark and I are boring. We've settled into old couple status." She pouts. "I don't know what you want to hear. I mean he brought a box of chocolates over to my house last week because I was on my period."

"Mark is the sweetest," I coo.

"Yeah, I'm glad he's my first boyfriend." Raina smiles. There's a brief pause before Raina squeals again. "We can finally do double dates!"

"Raina, we haven't even been on an actual date yet." I point out.

Raina rolls her eyes. "Those project adventures or whatever you call them *are* dates."

"Oh hush. You know those were for school." Even I know I'm lying.

"You should write a thank you letter to Mrs. Katz." She bursts into laughter. "Gosh, I'm so funny." Her laugh makes me laugh. Before long, my mom knocks on my wall to get me to shut up which only makes us laugh harder.

Once the laughter ceases, I ask, "Have you talked to Elise?"

"Nope. She needs to take time and realize how her actions affect others," Raina says matter-of-factly.

I can't stop my frown. "I feel like I betrayed her first. I mean, I went after a guy that she told me she liked from the first day. Then every time she tries to apologize, I run away."

"Technically, you met him first, and you forget that he doesn't like her. He likes *you*. It hurt way more for her to insinuate that you were ugly, especially when we all know your struggle with self-image. You don't owe her anything."

"Thanks Raina. Seriously." I focus my gaze on the screen. "I'm sorry that I broke our friend group apart."

"Not your fault. Besides, the people who are meant to be in your life will be in it," Raina quotes.

"Wow, you're so inspirational." I tease.

"Yeah, my mom is in her Pinterest phase, and I've kind of caught on. Next time you come by the house, you will see Pinterest quotes all over the wall. She literally prints out every quote she comes across and frames them. She's obsessed!"

"You're kidding!"

"I'm not. Just look at what she's done to my room," Raina turns her camera to a wall covered with pictures of inspirational quotes. "Like doesn't she know that 'Live Laugh Love' is a meme now?"

"That's the funniest thing I've seen all week." I cackle. It's like laughter is my high. When I come off it, I become somber again. "I hope our friend group can survive this. I miss them." I sigh. "I wish I could just suck it up and listen to Elise's apology so we can move on."

"I miss them too, but I think this time to self-reflect is necessary. It's normal for people to fall out. In fact, it's expected."

"But I just never thought it would happen to us."

It's a Tuesday when Elise and I speak to each other for the first time. Approaching our adjacent lockers with blonde hair in a claw clip, a sweatshirt, and flare leggings, she looks effortlessly pretty, as usual.

Instead of staring at my feet to avoid eye contact and walking away quickly like I usually do, I stay in the same spot and look at her.

"Hi." Elise's eyes are wide.

"Hi." I say feebly.

She looks at me again before she walks away, but says nothing else. I guess she's not trying to apologize anymore. But it's still the first verbal exchange that we've had since the winter formal so I feel a mixture of happiness and anger.

I'm so distracted by our encounter that I walk past the art classroom. Then I have to make a U-turn in the middle of the hallway like a complete idiot. The only plus is I get to see Slater.

He smiles when he sees me. "Hey you."

My heart plays a drum riff, and I forget all my issues. "Hey."

He pulls a yellow party blower out of his bookbag and blows into it. "Happy presentation day!"

"Where did you even get that?" I snicker.

"I might've dropped by the dollar store before school this morning."

My face breaks into a smile. "You're adorable."

"I know." He shrugs.

"I cannot believe the art project is almost over. It feels like just yesterday when you forced me to ride that behemoth of a roller coaster." I remember everything about that day. But that's not saying much because I remember everything that has ever happened between us and I replay it in my head. *Constantly*.

"Yeah, time really does fly." He gets up. When he returns, he has a canvas in his hands for the final part of our project of painting our post fear feelings. "Can I split the canvas in half this time?" he asks. He looks so adorable that I take a mental picture. This is how I will remember him, with brown locks over his forehead, pouting lips, and thunderstorm colored puppy dog eyes.

"Yes, but only because you look so freaking adorable right now."

"Wow, that brings the adorable count to what? Two?"

"Enjoy the compliments while they last." I playfully roll my eyes. "They only happen when I'm in a good mood." What I don't mention is that I'm always in a good mood around him.

"I mean, thanks, I guess. I'd rather be called handsome, good-kisser, that sort of thing you know?" He draws a line, but then he backtracks on his words. "You know what, screw toxic masculinity, adorable is perfect." I remember again why I like this boy so much.

"Look, I did it!" He drops his sharpie and reaches for a high five.

"I know this is going to bring the adorable count to three, but that was really adorable," I return his high five.

"Technically, it brought the adorable count to four."

"Oh, shush you." I playfully punch his arm.

He raised his arms in defense before focusing his attention on painting his side of the canvas red.

After watching him paint for a while, I speak up. "You know, I'm kind of emotional now. It's the end of a chapter."

"Don't be, we have so many more chapters in front of us." He looks up from his painting to wink at me.

While he returns to painting, I place my hand under my chin and doze off into the land of make believe. It was my favorite land, until I discovered that reality might be even better.

Slater slides the canvas over to me. His half is red with splatters of green, yellow, and white paint. Despite the unique color combination, it works. The speckles of white paint are like tiny rays of hope. "Okay, I'm done, now it's your turn. Hurry up, we have five minutes until we have to present."

I jokingly glare at him. "This is your fault. If you didn't take so long to paint, I'd have more than five minutes."

"Oops, sorry! I really got into it."

Adorable.

With increments of white in blue paint, I keep dipping my brush and flicking my wrist over the canvas to create what I hope looks like an ocean instead of some random blue and white blob.

"You feel like the ocean after facing your fears?" He peeks over my shoulder.

"Yeah, like I'm free and bound by nothing. I'm too powerful to be trapped. I'm the freaking ocean." It's not what I actually feel, but more what I *aspire* to feel. I promise myself that one day, I will feel like the ocean.

"That's awesome! Mine doesn't have as cool of a message as yours. He frowns at his side.

"It's beautiful, and it does mean something. We faced some of our fears! If I do say so myself, that's one of the bravest things anyone can do. Maybe we'll face the rest of our fears together some day." I regret it immediately afterwards. Why am I always so assuming? There's a good chance that we'll become glorified strangers after this project.

"We absolutely will," He reaches underneath the table to squeeze my hand. I look up at him and beam. The air feels like a thousand, tiny fireball explosions, and all I can think is that it's moments like these that they write books about.

But of course, these moments are always interrupted. In my case, it's Mrs. Katz and her shrill voice. "Okay everyone, it is time to present! While everyone was working on last minute touches, I put your names into a name generator," she pauses like she's expecting applause or compliments for doing her job. When she doesn't get any, she huffs and projects the name generator onto the whiteboard. "Let's see who is going first." The name wheel is sent into a colorful frenzy when Mrs. Katz clicks the space bar. As the wheel slows down near our names, I close my eyes and pray that it doesn't land on us.

Mrs. Katz announces, "Isla and Slater, you guys are first!" And I swear that I die a little on the inside.

Crap. Crap. Crap. Can I pretend to faint to get out of this? Or better yet, can I make myself faint? I wonder what the process is.

Slater interrupts my train of thoughts. "No doubts, okay?"

I roll my eyes, "No doubts." I'm slightly impressed at how calm I sound, especially when I'm freaking the crap out. I can feel and hear my heart beating everywhere, and sweat collects in beads on the back of my neck. I'm terrified I will mess up and everyone will laugh and throw tomatoes at me. I mean isn't that how it worked in Shakespeare's day?

"Do you want to do the introduction and speak your half first?" he asks.

"Sure." *No, I don't want to. I want to not do this presentation period.*

When Slater starts walking to the front of the classroom with our canvases, I have no choice but to follow him. As my eyes dart nervously across my classmates' faces, I try my best not to freak out. It doesn't work that well though, because here I am, freaking out.

"Umm, well hi, guys," I stiffly wave to the class. "So, we did our art project on finding the true meaning of fear. Umm, we investigated this meaning by facing some of our fears and depicted how we felt before and after facing the fears." I gesture awkwardly at the canvases in Slater's hand and mentally high-five myself for not crying. *Go me!*

"This canvas is our depiction of our feelings pre fear facing." Slater raises the half greyscale and half abstract painting in his right hand. "The other one is how we felt post fear facing." He raises the other canvas. My hands are shaking despite not holding anything, but here Slater is, holding two paintings with perfectly steady hands.

How is he not freaking out?

Somehow, I find the nerve to chime in. "Basically, we discovered that overthinking is the cause of fear, and that fear is a liar." *Gosh I'm such a hypocrite.*

"Unhealthy excessive fear isn't beneficial. All it does is hinder us from achieving our greatest potential. This is the true meaning of fear," Slater concludes.

I add an awkward "Um, yeah," at the end.

The class applauds loudly, even though our presentation wasn't good enough to warrant *that* big of a reaction. It's probably because Slater is attractive and popular. I'm just glad that it's over with no tomatoes thrown.

"Go Isla!" Camila cheers. I smile at my previous seat partner.

"A great start to presentations. Thank you, Slater, and Isla. Please return to your seats now," Mrs. Katz shouts over the claps.

In our seats, Slater whispers to me, "We did good."

"It was a bit short, wasn't it?" I ask. The familiar clutch of overthinking pulls me under again. It's like how Angelica Schuyler once sang about never being satisfied.

"Yeah, but it's an art project. Hopefully Mrs. Katz will just give everyone a one hundred. Art is basically a participation grade," Slater replies, calm and steady as always.

I shrug and let it go. "I guess." I mean, it's not like I check the grade portal anymore anyways.

"And to celebrate, we should take a subway trip down to Times Square after school today," he continues.

"Too touristy."

"Exactly! We're going to have a bona fide New York day." He grins.

"That sounds kind of like a date."

"Maybe because it is a date."

Just like that, my mood lifts, and a smile creeps onto my face. "But why can't we just take your car."

"It's hard to find parking, and we want the whole tourist experience, you know? We have to see New York City from shiny eyes and be oblivious to all the bad," he winks.

"I still have to ask my parents if I can go. What if they say no?"

"Tell them it's a part of the project. I mean, it technically is. Post project celebration still counts as part of the project," he concludes.

"Makes sense," I laugh. "How do your parents not care what you do?"

"They trust me to not be an idiot, and they have a phone tracking app." His shrug is expressive.

"Valid." I nod, unsure of what else to say.

Then the bell rings, and I flinch. That went by fast! I feel bad that I didn't pay attention to the other presentations. *Who do I think I am? The main character?* My ego needs a big reality check.

CHAPTER 15

My parents ended up agreeing, so here I am, in Slater's multiple car garage. Once again.

"Should we go greet your parents?" I ask.

"They're at work. Besides, if they were here and we dropped in to greet them, it would be at least an hour before we left. In fact, we might not even be able to leave at all. We were lucky to escape last time." He shivers, genuine fear loud on his face. "I don't think it's smart to push our luck."

I laugh. "Your parents are great."

"Whatever you say."

"They are!"

He raises his eyebrows and shrugs. "Yeah, I guess they are. Don't tell them that I admitted this, though. They will hold it over my head."

I smile until it hurts.

"Well, ready to go?" He offers his hand to me.

I take it, and let him guide me onto the street. I don't know exactly what we are. Friends? Or more? I just like that we can hold hands.

Pretty brownstones, the occasional New York tree, and the bright, blue sky encircles me. I have this weird desire to twirl. I won't even be surprised if birds start flying around me and a musical soundtrack starts playing in the background. It's like this romanticized version of life that I've had in my head has become real.

"My goodness, your neighborhood is nice." I whistle in admiration. I mean what am I expecting? It is the Upper East Side after all.

"Yeah, and our neighbors are pretty nice too. Some are less talkative than others, but who cares? In the end we're all just people trying to find our way in life," Slater reflects, and he has his thinking face on. Scrunched eyebrows and all.

I pause before laughing. "How did you manage to turn talking about your neighbors into something philosophical?"

He laughs along with me. "Honestly, I don't know either. That art project presentation has me messed up and reconsidering life."

The laughter ceases, and I don't know what to do. It was easy before because we used to be just friends. Now I'm in uncharted waters. Should I tell a joke? Should I try to kiss him? Why isn't there a guidebook or a YouTube tutorial?

Once we swipe our metro cards at the subway station, curiosity overtakes the overthinking. "Why were you at a subway station in Queens on the first day we met? I mean not that I'm not grateful. Trust me, I'm *super* grateful."

"I still hadn't gotten my car yet, and my mom wanted me to take her chicken pot pie to my grandparents. They live really close to you actually."

"Well thank goodness for pot pie. Without it, none of this would've happened."

"Do you really believe that? I think we'd still be this close even if you didn't spill coffee on me." He winks at me.

"Don't remind me. That was so awkward." I cringe. "But yeah. You probably wouldn't have been curious enough to get to know me."

"You're pretty, I would've definitely tried to get to know you." He winks.

I blush. "Liar."

He looks at me, deep and intense, like I'm the biggest mystery in life. "My goodness Isla, when will you finally realize how beautiful you are?"

I send him a feeble smile. "I'm working on it. I can't just reverse years of hating myself in one day. I wish I could, but I can't." As much as fairy tales want to push that love can change everything, it just isn't true.

He throws an arm around my shoulder and pulls me closer. I get on the tippy toes of my dirty sneakers to lay my head on his shoulder and think back on our first subway trip together. Past me wouldn't have even dreamed that I would become *this* close to this amazing person. Thank you, spilt coffee!

The Q train thunders towards us, and the too familiar female robotic voice announces, "This is a Manhattan bound N train. The next stop is Times Square-42nd Street." All the seats on the train are taken so Slater and I hold on to a metal pole next to an old man.

When the train starts moving, the old man mutters under his breath, "Chink." I almost think that I imagined it, but then he repeats it. Again, and again, and again.

The air leaves my lungs, but I'm so tired of feeling weak and embarrassed. I'm so tired of betraying myself. When Slater opens his mouth to speak, I raise my hand and look at him, communicating "I got this" with my eyes.

Slater beams and mouths, "I'm proud of you."

"Go back home, Ling Ling. Maybe I need to say it in Chinese. Ching chong, ching chong," the old man spits the mockery out with pure hatred.

I suck in a deep breath for confidence. "I feel sorry for you. I feel sorry for your terrible, uninformed view of life. I was actually born in America, but even if I wasn't, I'd still have the right to call this country my home. Immigrants *deserve* the right. Do you know how difficult it is to come here? My parents have tried their best to shield me from most of the harsh realities, but it's hard when people hate crime you and shout slurs everywhere you go." I chuckle humorlessly. "You're so beyond privileged, and you don't even realize it. No one's going to have a 'bad day' and shoot up your business. This is my burden to bear, and I wouldn't wish this burden on anyone. Not even you."

Slater squeezes my shoulder and I place my hand on top of his hand, silently thanking him for his support. "I didn't choose to be an Asian American, but man, I'm so freaking proud to be one. My only regret is that it took me so long to realize it. You, on the other hand, chose to be racist." I shrug like I don't care. "That's not something *anyone* should be proud of."

When I finish speaking, the train car is utterly silent. I turn around to stares and recording phones. One person begins clapping, and soon after, others follow suit.

"You tell him, girl!" someone hollers.

My face flushes. When did everyone start paying attention? Was I really that loud?

The old man is seething, but before he can splutter another racist remark, the robotic voice announces, "This is Times Square-42nd Street. Transfer is available to the 1, 2, 3, 5, 7, N, Q, R, and W trains."

On the way out, Slater leans down to whisper in my ear, "You amaze me."

I don't let the racist old man dampen my mood. Instead, I have the freaking time of my life. I imagine that this is what it feels like to be high.

Time Square smothers us with its flashy advertisements and money scamming Avengers. I swear Spiderman has attempted to coerce us into a picture about a hundred times now. Slater and I eventually end up at a subpar, overpriced Italian restaurant, definitely a tourist trap, but at least we're protected from Spiderman.

Then we go ice skating at Rockefeller Center and discover that we both suck at ice skating. Yes, even Slater. I was shocked too. After far too many falls, we call it quits. I let Slater buy me a street hot dog, and then we find a bench to sit on. My cheeks hurt from smiling so much, but I can't stop. All I want to do is jump up and down and scream, "I love life!" I hope this night never ends.

"Hey," Slater says out of nowhere.

"Hey." I laugh, looking around.

There's a brief pause before he speaks again. "Will you be my girlfriend?"

My jaw drops. Is this actually happening? What is life? I look at him for a moment, eyes widened and no words in my head, before I hug him and squeal. "Yes, yes, yes! Of course!"

He beams at me. "You know, you really scared me for a second there, Isla Wu."

"My mind stops working when shocked." I grin. "A thousand times yes, Slater Wesbrook. Scratch that, a million freaking times yes."

"A million freaking times, huh? You must really like me." His eyes twinkle. They are the stars in this starless, city night.

"Yeah, a million freaking times," I confirm. "I must really like you."

Slater pulls me into a kiss, and I can feel his smile on my lips.

Before going to bed, I used to make scenarios in my head about what it would be like to have a boyfriend. This is nothing like my imagination. It's way better. A million freaking times better.

School is a whole different experience with a boyfriend.

Slater continues to sit with me and Raina at lunch, but other people have also moved to join us, including Lucy and Connor. I don't think I've ever spoken to some of these people in my life, but now we're all crowded into one tiny, bathroom-adjacent table. It's funny how life works.

Today is one of those rare days when Raina and I arrive to an empty lunch table.

"Well, we're freakishly early," Raina observes.

"Yeah. Isn't it weird that we've become honorary members of the popular group somehow?"

"What do you mean, 'somehow'?" Raina deadpans. "You're dating one of the most popular guys in school. Of course we're freaking inducted."

I laugh. "Raina!"

"It's true, but I'm not mad. You guys are super cute, and I'm collecting my favor by forcing you and Slater to go on a double date with me and Mark."

"You just said you weren't mad."

"Yeah, but that doesn't mean I don't want a favor. I'll take whatever I can get so–" Raina looks behind me.

I know his presence like the back of my hand, maybe even better. "Hey." Slater kisses my cheek.

A grin appears instantly on my face. "Hey." Out of the corner of my eye, I can see Raina making kissy faces at me.

Not long after Slater, others start flooding the table until we're all crowded with barely an inch of space between each other. On top of that, I have a direct view of Elise pursing her lips. Since the news of Slater and I spread around the school, she has stopped acknowledging me in the hallway. It kind of really hurts.

"I'm going to the bathroom," I tell Slater in the midst of a conversation about an upcoming party that I won't be invited to.

Slater nods with a frown. As I get up to leave, he whispers in my ear, "I'm sorry."

"About what?"

His eyes point towards the table. "All of this."

"I don't blame you. It's just the Slater Effect." I smile.

His eyebrows are scrunched, but I walk away before he has the chance to ask me what I meant.

In the bathroom stall, some girls are gossiping in hushed tones. My ears only perk up when they mention Slater and my names. "Did you know that Slater is dating Isla?" One girl asks.

"Who is Isla?" Another girl responds. I roll my eyes.

I assume someone has pulled up a picture of me because the next thing I hear is, "Really, her?"

My face heats up and tears prickle in my eyes, but this isn't the first time I've heard this. This exact conversation has happened in different fonts, in *all* settings. Even the freshmen are talking about it, so you'd think I'd be used to it by now.

Slater waits for me in front of my locker after the bell rings.

"Hey.," I raise my eyebrows.

"Do you think you can come over for dinner?" Slater asks. "My mom has been bugging me ever since she met you."

"Straight to the point." I remark with a grin. "But yeah, I'd love to. It's kind of endearing that she wants to get to know me so badly."

Slater smiles at me. "You just charm everyone you meet, don't you?"

I roll my eyes. "Have we never met?"

Fifteen minutes later, I'm hiking up a staircase with sweat collecting in dews on my forehead because of both my lack of athleticism and nervousness.

"What if they hate me?"

"Isla, they already know and love you. The day you guys met, I came home to so many compliments and questions about you."

"But we didn't really *talk*, you know? What if they realize that they hate my personality? I'm super awkward and–" He kisses me, interrupting my sentence and halting all of my thoughts.

When we pull away the left corner of his lip lifts up as he offers me his hand. "Trust me, they adore you. Now, let's do this."

Jen is reading a magazine in the living room. When she spots us, she takes off her glasses and stands up. "Isla! Come give me a hug."

Slater mouths, "I told you so."

Jen has perfected the hug, down to the precise amount of squeeze and proximity. My nerves go away, and when she retreats, my arms miss her light pressure.

"When Slater told me you could make it, I was overjoyed!" Jen beams.

"She really was." William appears beside Slater. "She ran to the recipe books and flipped through them so fast that I thought she would get a papercut. It's a miracle she didn't."

We laugh. A fuzzy feeling arises within me, and I'm happy.

"Thank you, guys, for having me."

"Of course, dear! Now you and Slater go hang out while William and I try to prepare this dinner." Jen waves us away.

"Do you need any help?" I offer, despite the fact that the only thing I can cook is grilled cheese.

"You are so sweet, but I think we're good." She reassures me with a smile.

When we're in Slater's room, I let curiosity overtake me. "Do your parents not have a cook?" I splutter, "I mean, I just assumed they would because of how nice this house is. I don't have a cook. Umm, never mind, forget that I asked that."

Slater chuckles heartily. "Isla, you're so over stressed today. No, they do not have a cook, but that's mostly because they love cooking together." He tucks his face on the crook of my neck.

"I love this side of you." I press my cheek against his. As nervous as I am about everything else, I'm not nervous about him. Well, at least not anymore. It's something so dazzlingly comfortable and great, and I don't think I'll ever feel like this with anyone else.

"I love that I can finally do this." Slater sprinkles kisses on my jaw.

I'm so thrilled. All I want to do is declare to the world that this is *my* boyfriend.

A good forty minutes later, Jen calls us down for a delicious pasta dinner with chocolate cake for dessert. Talk and laughter flows easily, and they really do make me feel like I am a part of the Wesbrook family.

"Thanks for coming." Jen gifts me with another hug as we get ready to leave.

"Thanks for inviting me I had the greatest time."

"You must come back and have dinner again with us soon," William says.

"Just send me a date and I will be there," I laugh.

Slater wraps an arm around me and as we walk downstairs to his car, he asks, "Do you have something to tell me?"

"Are you really going to make me say it?" I ask, snuggling closer to his arm.

"Yup."

"You were right. Happy?"

"Very." His smirk is smug.

At my house, both of my parents are standing outside with crossed arms and glares on their faces. It's then that I realize that I didn't tell my parents where I was going. Oops.

"Why didn't you answer our calls?" My dad yells. "Where were you?"

"Sorry I had my phone off. I was having dinner at a friend's–"

"Whose car is that and who is driving?" My mom interrupts me.

Crap I didn't want them to find out so soon. Or ever. But as luck would have it, here we are. "Um, mom and dad, this is umm...this is my boyfriend, Slater." I mentally prepare myself for the yelling.

Their eyes widen in shock, and that's when Slater steps out to introduce himself. "Hello Mr. and Mrs. Wu, I'm Slater Wesbrook." *Oh gosh. Can I disappear right now? Please.*

"My last name is Huang," my mom corrects, and Slater's face flushes a little. "But nice meet you."

She turns to my dad and asks in Chinese, "How did our daughter get such a handsome boyfriend?" To that, my dad shrugs. Jeez, thanks mom and dad.

"Thanks for get Isla home safe," my dad says. I don't let myself get embarrassed over their broken English. Finally, I see things from their side, and I *admire* them.

"Of course." Slater nods.

"Do you want come to our *Dongzhi* Festival? Lot of family going to be there, and I know everyone want to meet Isla's boyfriend." Mom smirks.

"I'd love to." Slater smiles his famous dimpled smile.

"Good. Isla, text you later," Mom says.

Dad nods once more and then my parents walk back to the house, shooting each other looks along the way. That was way less yelling and tears than I expected.

"Dang, Wesbrook. An invite from my mom in less than five minutes?" I tease him. "And you claim that I'm the charmer."

"I guess it's my turn to be nervous," he jokes in response, but I can tell he's serious. "Do you think they're staring at us through the window?"

"Oh, for sure."

"Dang it, I really wanted to kiss you."

I beam and sneak a kiss on his cheek. "Bye."

"Bye." I expect him to get in his car and leave, but he doesn't. Instead, he pulls me into a hug.

And as I watch him finally drive away, I realize that this boy will most definitely be the end of me.

CHAPTER 16

I want to be anywhere other than this too hot math classroom. Mr. Walter stomps around before placing another graded test on my desk. It's a fail, of course, but this time, it comes with an endearing, handwritten note. "See me after class."

And I don't even get upset anymore, I'm desensitized. It's kind of funny how when something happens to you repeatedly, all the emotions go away. It becomes predictable and just another part of life.

I zone out the rest of class. I mean, even when I try to focus, my brain won't process it, so what's the point? However, I do stay behind to talk to Mr. Walter. The teacher's pet in me hasn't disappeared yet.

"Isla, please grab a seat. This won't take long, but I'll write you a note for your next class just in case." Mr. Walter scribbles on an orange sticky note. Once I sit down, Mr. Walter speaks up again. "You probably have a faint idea of why you're here."

I shrug and cross my arms.

Mr. Walter scrutinizes me with narrowed eyes before cutting to the chase. "You're failing my class, and according to your past math teachers, this is very out of character." *Gosh, now he has been speaking to my past teachers?*

"Is there anything going on at home?" And now he's going to be my shrink. *Great.*

"No, everything is fine. Precalculus is hard."

Mr. Walter looks at me again before he gives up. "All right then." He hands me an excused tardy pass. "I strongly recommend you come to office hours."

I shrug again, but of course, I don't come to office hours. And it's not just precalculus. I've been failing all of my classes.

"Wesbrook, are you sure you can't come to Megan's party tonight?" Elliot asks.

Slater slings an arm around my shoulder. "Isla and I are hanging out today." Regret swirls through me, like a category five hurricane. Am I keeping him from his life?

"Dang, I'll miss you, bro." Elliot slams his locker door shut.

"Now don't get all sentimental on me, Choi," Slater jokes.

Elliot rolls his eyes and mouths, "Screw you."

"Are you sure you don't want to go to the party?" I ask once Elliot is gone.

"I'd much rather hang with you." Slater winks.

"I feel like I'm taking you away from your friends. I insist that you go."

"I promise you're not, but fine, I'll go on one condition." He smirks and his eyes crinkle. I have a feeling that I'm not going to like whatever comes out of his mouth next.

"What condition?" I play along.

"That you come with me."

I knew it. I raise my eyebrows. "I'm not invited."

"Everyone is invited. It's an open party," Slater's eyes dance with mischief as he tilts his head at me.

I giggle and push his arm playfully. "They claim it's an open party, but what they really mean is that it's only open to the cool kids."

"Please come with me." Slater pouts, shooting me puppy eyes. I've never encountered such effective puppy eyes before, and that's coming from someone who once thought puppy eyes were *her* signature look.

"Fine, but I have a condition too." And that's how Raina and Mark end up in the backseat of Slater's car, scrunching their noses up at us when Slater kisses my cheek.

My face flushes red. "Oh my gosh, guys please stop staring. Or better yet, just get out of the car."

"We're being nice and waiting on you." Raina smirks, fluttering her eyes. "And it's kind of fascinating how touchy you guys are."

Slater coughs, and my face reddens even more. "But you guys are dating too," I manage to splutter.

Mark laughs. "I think what Raina means is that we're different types of couples. You guys are more affectionate."

I swear that I die a little inside. "Okay, conversation over. Can we please go?"

"Yes, please." Slater rushes to open his door. "They're going to make fun of us the entire night, aren't they?"

"Oh, most definitely. And they'll laugh if we trip. They're lowkey a sadistic couple."

Slater and I share the same grimace while Raina's laughter echoes behind us, even in the elevator ride up to Megan's penthouse.

Once the elevator drops us off, Slater knocks on a dark wooden door and some guy I don't know opens it. "Wesbrook," he slurs, eyes widening in recognition as he reaches out to give Slater a handshake. "Hey man, welcome."

The hit of booze, weed, and loud music is instant. The room is packed, bodies pressed together in a haze of cigarette smoke and flashing neon lights. Everywhere I look, groups of people are clustered around couches, laughing, and chatting loudly, some with drinks in hand, others leaning in close to each other. The bass from the music vibrates through the floor, rattling the expensive furniture and making the air feel thick and alive with energy. Wow! This is kind of like a scene out of *Gossip Girl*. I guess the show was based on reality–well, the reality of the cool kids. My parents would kill me if they knew where I was.

More people are tripping over themselves to greet Slater. Raina and Mark are talking about who knows what, and I am quickly discovering that this is not my scene. When I spot Elise and Aisha crowded in a corner, surrounded by people with beers in their hands, I instantly avert my eyes.

"I didn't know they went to these parties." My eyes widen in shock.

"Who?" Raina shouts over the music.

"Elise and Aisha."

Raina laughs. "Why do you think they could never hang out on Fridays?" I shouldn't be hurt, but I am. Why didn't they ever invite us, or at least say where they were going? Did I ever really know them at all?

I stare out of one of the many glass floor-to-ceiling windows. The clear weather has been replaced by rain that encircles the city. It's kind of like nature's carousel. But as much as I love watching the rain, I'd love to fit in even more. I wish I could be one of those people, swaying to loud music with their eyes closed, hands in the air, and no care in the world.

I'm so fixated that I don't even realize that Slater is next to me until he speaks. "Hey."

"Hey. Everyone looks so happy." I was so jealous.

"Not everything is as it seems. For some of them, it's an escape. They don't want to be here, but they know of nothing else that will give them relief." Slater says with scrunched eyebrows and glazed over eyes.

I don't know what else to say besides "Oh."

"Want to get out of here?" Slater asks.

"You know me so well." I smile.

Slater grins back. "This isn't my scene either. Not anymore." I want to ask what he means by that, but I refrain.

We tell Raina and Mark that we will be waiting for them in the car before sprinting off like fugitives. Some people raise their eyebrows at us, but weirdly enough, I don't care. The minute the rain hits my face is when I can finally breathe normally. I pause and stick my tongue out to catch raindrops.

Slater's laughter reverberates through the empty street. "You really are something, aren't you, Isla Wu?"

I beam and reach my hand out to him. "No doubts, Slater Wesbrook!"

Slater twirls me around and pulls me in for a kiss. The rain pours around and on us, my hair and clothes are drenched, and my heels are slippery, but I'm deliriously happy. It's a scene straight out of the movies, but somehow, even better. And it's then that I know that he has engraved himself a permanent spot on my heart.

When we finally make it to the car, our clothes soak the seats. We look at each other and laugh. Then the post-happiness somber hits, and it's quiet. "What did you mean earlier when you said that this isn't your scene anymore?" I gather the confidence to ask.

Slater smiles again, but unlike his other smiles, this one doesn't reach his eyes. "I fell in with the wrong crowd after Willow died." He takes a breath. "I got into all sorts of things, and then there was this hospital scare. My parents couldn't bear the thought of losing another kid so they forced me into therapy, changed my phone number, and put me in a new school."

"Did it work?" I ask softly, my voice trembling under the weight of his words. My chest tightens, aching for the boy he was and the pain he carried alone. I want to tell him it's okay to have hurt, to have been lost, but the words stick to my throat.

"Yeah. I'm really glad they did it. My only regret was breaking their hearts. Gosh, all I could think about was myself and my pain, and I didn't pay attention to their pain."

"I think there's something wrong with–" I start to say, but I'm interrupted by Raina and Mark knocking on the windows.

Slater unlocks the car. "What were you going to say?"

This time it's my turn for a smile that doesn't reach my eyes. "Nothing."

Two hours before the *Dongzhi* festival dinner, Slater video calls me. "Should I bring anything? I've been researching, but all the internet seems to care about is Chinese New Year. It's not fair that some holidays get to be the dominant holiday. Like gosh, Easter can be just as great as Christmas, and *Dongzhi* Festival can be just as great as Chinese New Year. You know, I blame the movie industry for this," he scratches his neck nervously. It's adorable how dedicated he is.

"You don't need to bring anything except your pretty self."

"Are you sure?"

"Yes."

"Can I come over early? If I stay home any longer, I'm going to freak myself out."

"Of course." I love that he's nervous.

Thirty minutes later, he is at my doorstep, fidgeting with a red tie.

"You clean up nice." Inside, I'm jumping up and down and squealing. I love that I get to share this with him, but I'd be lying if I said that I wasn't a little excited to show him off.

"Thanks, and you look beautiful, as usual," he says.

"You have to tell me that." I roll my eyes playfully.

"It's a fact."

"Technically, it's an opinion."

"It's a fact." he grins at me while taking his shoes off to enter the house. "Can I help with anything?"

"I mean, you could try if you want my mom to yell at me about making a guest do things. She'll come up with this whole speech, you'll love it."

He laughs. "I would love to hear it. But seriously, I really want to help out."

"I'm serious too! You can help out by relaxing and enjoying yourself."

He pretends to pout.

My dad beckons me over to the kitchen, and I start to walk away until Slater calls my name.

"Are you sure you don't want any help?" Slater cups his hands around his mouth to yell. We're, at most, three feet apart from each other.

I giggle and mimic him. "Yes!" An hour later, the first wave of guests arrive, including my grandparents. They don't greet me, and I don't make an effort to greet them. My grandparents have never liked me, even as a kid. Needless to say, it made grandparents' day really uncomfortable.

With focused hawk eyes, my mom marches towards us. "Slater, I'm so happy to see you." I'm surprised that she didn't spot Slater until now.

"I wouldn't miss it for the world." he looks at me and I swear his eyes sparkle.

"Suck-up," I mutter under my breath.

He smirks at me before leaning down to whisper in my ear, "It's your mom. I want her to like me."

My mom claps her hands with delight, and rushes off to grab family members and several "aunties." Eventually a circle of people forms around Slater and I.

One of the aunties blinks at me before saying in Chinese, "Isla, you have grown so quickly. You were just a little girl yesterday."

"Yeah." I fake laugh. I don't even recognize her.

"You got very *pàng*, huh?" Once again, this word comes to attack me. *Pàng. Fat.*

The group of ladies, including my *own* mother, giggles with her. Instantly, my mood sours, and my eyes focus on the ground. Slater, even though he doesn't understand a word being said, squeezes my hand.

"She won't exercise," my mom explains.

"A healthy diet is the key! All vegetables and no meat," another auntie offers.

"I keep telling her this, but she won't listen. She's stubborn like her dad." Then my mom switches to English for Slater. "This Isla boyfriend, Slater."

Slater only smiles at them politely, and my heart gushes. I'm totally selfish for thinking this, but I love that he doesn't say that it's nice to meet them.

One lady shoots me a thumbs up, before saying in Chinese, "My daughter Rachel's boyfriend certainly does not look like that." The group laughs again, and my mom has this self-satisfied smile on her face. It's always a competition with my mom and her friends to see who has the better life, whose child attends the more prestigious college, whose husband takes them on a better vacation. At least I finally gave her something to brag about.

"If you and Isla break up, I have a daughter." Another auntie winks. My jaw drops. The audacity is insane.

"Sorry, excuse us. I just remembered, me and Isla have to do something." Slater guides me away from the circle, and we hear a collective groan of disappointment. It's definitely not me that they're going to miss. Once we're out of earshot, he whispers, "Wow, they're really forward."

"Yeah."

He looks at me with a raised eyebrow. I stare back at him for a second before giving up. "They basically talked about how fat I am, but it's fine, I'm used to it."

Slater shakes his head and wraps his arms around me. "Don't listen to them. You are perfect," he says into my hair.

I shrug. I really don't understand why he chose me—and obviously the world doesn't either—but I'm thankful that he did.

"Isla, who is this?"

I turn to find my grandma hand in hand with my grandpa. I guess Slater is the main event this year. "This is my boyfriend, Nai Nai," I say to my grandma.

My grandpa huffs, and then they walk away.

"You're standing in a room full of people who don't like me," I try to joke.

His eyes crinkle as he hugs me. "I like you."

"You're in the minority." I laugh self-depreciatingly. *Gosh, it's all so messed up.*

My little cousins run through us, and their parents yell at them to slow down. Then my mom calls everyone over to a giant table that I never see except on holidays. There's so many plates of food that they overlap each other. My eyes narrow in on the steaming soup dumplings and tang yuan, little rice balls filled with sesame goodness.

After many, *many* refills of food, I'm slouched over with my head on the table. Through the corner of my eye, I can see my mom forcing a container of leftovers towards Slater.

"Take home to parents," she orders.

"Wow, thank you. They'll be so excited."

She gives him a close-lipped smile before speeding off to who knows where. Then it's just me and Slater in the dining room.

"Hey, sleepy." He teases.

"I'm not sleepy," I protest, but then I prove him right with a yawn.

He chuckles, and kisses me on the forehead. "I have to go, unfortunately."

"No, don't go. Can't you stay?"

"I don't want to, but my mom has already called me twice." I give him puppy eyes, which makes Slater laugh again. "Okay, fine. Five more minutes."

In the middle of the night, unexpected numbness hits me like a typhoon. Slowly creeping up and then all at once, I'm drowning and it's too late to swim. This isn't supposed to happen. I am not supposed to feel like this in one of the happiest stages in my life. I am not supposed to feel empty when I have a freaking boyfriend.

I force myself to check my grades. They're all Fs.

The tears start to flow, and I sob silently into the night.

CHAPTER 17

I cannot be alone anymore.

All that has been circulating in my head is how much I screwed everything up. No college is going to want me now. *What am I going to do? What am I going to do? What am I going to do?* I refuse to deal with this. I cannot deal with this. The only thing I can do is cry, but even tears have their limits.

I'm not even mediocre anymore. I'm a freaking failure. I curl up into a ball, and I rock back and forth. *What am I going to do?*

Then I realize that it's too late to do anything, so I distract myself. If I can give myself a few moments of reprieve, I'm going to freaking do it. The reality hurts too much.

Me: *Hey, r u doing anything today?*

Slater texts me back immediately:

Slater: *Nope. Want to hang?*

Me: *Duh*

Slater: *Omw to your house. Be there in 30.*

In exactly thirty minutes, I see his car outside my window and the pain alleviates. I can't believe I took all the happiness for granted before. Only now, in my darkest place, do I understand.

I run down the stairs to hug him. "Hi!"

He picks me up and spins me around. "Hey, you."

Out of appreciation, I reach up to kiss Slater. "I miss you."

"I've missed you too in the two days we've been apart." He cracks a smile.

"Two days too long!"

"Two days too long," he agrees dutifully.

Thank God my parents are at work, or they'd be staring us down.

"So, what do you want to do?" Slater asks.

"Well, I was hoping you'd have the answer to that."

He laughs again. It's such a magical sound that I wish I could bottle it to keep with me forever. "How about Central Park?"

"Are we going to do another round of touristy dates?"

"Yup, unless–"

"Unless what?"

"Unless you want to ride another roller coaster." He smirks, eyes crinkling.

My grimace is immediate. "Nope. No way."

"That's what I thought."

"You know me so well."

"Don't you forget it," Slater winks. I know he's joking, but it's an inconceivable idea. I don't think I'll ever forget *anything* about him.

We park at his house, and he grabs a stuffed picnic basket from his trunk. Again, I'm reminded of how much he goes out of his way for me.

"You're so prepared." I teasingly chide. "And very assuming."

Slater grins toothily at me. "It's not like it's hard. You can be very indecisive."

I jokingly punch his arm, and he takes my hand. "You're not getting this back now." He jokes.

But Slater is true to his word, and holds onto my hand on the stroll to and through Central Park. There's a throng of picnickers we have to push past, but eventually, we find a spot underneath some oak trees. Once we finish laying down the pastel orange picnic blanket, I look at the sky. It's a perfect day with perfect clouds and a perfect blue sky, but deep inside, I think I prefer the chaos that comes with a rainy day.

I hear the opening and closing of the picnic basket, and seconds later, a bouquet of daisies appears in my sight. A smile so intense that my eyes start watering stretches across my face. "Slater Wesbrook, you shouldn't have."

He leans in to kiss my nose. "Only the best for my girl." *Oh my, gosh. Oh my, gosh. Oh my, gosh.*

I melt. I literally freaking melt. I swing my arms around his neck, and drag him in for a kiss. "You. Are. The. Greatest," I whisper into his lips between kisses.

"No. You." Even though a myriad of people surround us, it still feels like we're the only two people in the world. *How did I get so lucky?*

I swear that stars are in my eyes when I look at him. He pulls out what looks like a charcuterie board stuffed into plastic containers. Two turkey sandwiches, a plate of chocolate covered strawberries, napkins, bottles of iced water, and finally, a gigantic bottle of mayo. I look at him weirdly.

"I'm testing how much you actually love mayo," he teases.

"How did you know?" I ask, my eyes lighting up in surprise.

"You told me on the roller coaster."

"That was so long ago. How do you still remember that?"

"I have my ways," Slater winks at me.

"Well, for our next date, we should go get pineapple pizza."

His dual dimples popping out as he nods his head repeatedly. "Great idea, girlfriend."

"Thanks, boyfriend." I grab a cracker from the container and stack it with cheddar cheese.

"Do you only eat the crackers and cheese?" Slater banters.

"And the grapes!" I protest. "Not all of us can be a charcuterie snob." My pout only makes him laugh harder.

"Don't ever change, Isla Wu."

After finishing everything in the picnic basket, we lay down to stare at the sky together. It's blissful and great, but then the reality of my situation kicks in again and I feel an odd mixture of pain and numbness. I don't even know how that works. I thought I could avoid it. I thought I could distract myself. There's so many things I thought I could do.

Slater looks over at me. Maybe he said something, I'm not sure. These thoughts have me in an unflinching chokehold. I start to sweat.

"Isla, are you okay?"

I blink twice before I can give him an answer. "Yeah." *No.*

He tilts his head and raises an eyebrow. He doesn't believe me.

"I'm totally fine. You don't need to worry about me." I give him a thumbs up.

He continues staring at me, but he lets me off easy. "Isla, you know I'm here for you right? You can tell me *anything.*"

"Yeah." *I don't want to admit it out loud, but something is definitely wrong with me.*

Grades keep getting handed out as teachers scramble to calculate final averages before exams. This time, they're essays from history. It's yet another failing grade for me. But it's not like I was expecting anything different.

Out of the corner of my eye, I look at Raina's paper and envy curls inside me like a snake, wrapping itself around my organs and squeezing until I can't breathe anymore. I miss when I was failing and didn't care.

I think Raina has always been the person I was the most jealous of. Yes, I wish I had Elise's beauty and Aisha's confidence, but Raina always seemed like an elevated version of myself. She's smarter, she's prettier, she's skinnier. Isla 2.0. Or maybe I'm just a worse version of her, I don't know.

All I know is that sometimes, it's really freaking difficult to be her friend.

"Isla, what did you get?" Raina asks. I know her question stems from sheer curiosity, but gosh, it can be *so* annoying. I wish she failed and I was the one with the perfect grade.

"I failed." I shrug and try to hide all the emotions from my face.

Raina frowns and adapts a different tone of voice, one full of pity and sorrow. "I'm sorry. You'll do better next time, I'm sure of it."

I know she's trying to be friendly, but gosh, it sure can feel condescending. Because no, I won't do better next time, and it's no fault of hers, but still. I give her a tight smile. "Thanks."

I'm pushing her away, but I can't help myself.

A few days later, Raina catches me before I leave English class. "Why are you avoiding me?"

"What do you mean? I'm not avoiding you." *I am definitely avoiding her.*

Raina stares at me. "Stop lying."

"I'm not." *I am.*

"Isla, we've been friends for four years, do you really think that I don't know when you're lying? Your eyebrow twitch is a dead giveaway."

I try deep breaths to calm myself down, but it doesn't work. I erupt. "Okay fine. It's freaking hard to be around you Raina. Is that what you want to hear?"

Her eyes water, but she doesn't speak.

I turn around to leave. "I have to go to gym class."

Raina calls after me. "Since you hate being my friend so much, I free you from the burden."

Some people turn in the hallways to look at us, but honestly, I don't care anymore. Everything has gone to crap.

"Fine!" I shout with all my hurt and anger.

"Fine!"

But it's *not* freaking fine. I hate that I've pushed her away, I hate that I'm like this, I hate that I've ruined another good thing in my life.

CHAPTER 18

Slater and I have become inseparable. Or rather, I have been forcing him to hang out with me because I cannot be alone. We're sitting in his car right now, and Slater is drumming his fingers against the dashboard. I can't seem to talk to him, which is *insane* because he's easy-going, good-at-conversing Slater.

"So, I was thinking we should go watch a movie." Slater sits and twiddles his thumbs like he's nervous.

"I'm sorry, I'm just really not in the mood. Can we just hang out in your car?" I ask.

Slater's face falls and he lowers his eyes. "Yeah, that's fine. Next time?"

I wonder if he planned something and I just ruined it. An onslaught of guilt rushes through me. I put my hands on his cheeks and draw him in for a kiss because I don't know what else to do. He kisses me back. It's awesome like all his other kisses are, but it feels *different*. There's a shift between us, I know it, he knows it, but our lips remain attached until we run out of air.

Still, he is my flotation device, the only thing keeping me from drowning.

"Next time," I confirm after we pull away, but I don't know if I'm lying or not. I wish I could force myself to feel better for him, or at the very least, fake it.

It turns out that I was lying.

All of our dates have turned into car make out sessions which I know is my fault with the way I keep shutting him down and shutting him out. I want to be different, but I can't seem to control my actions. I know that's super contradictory to pretty much everything that science says about the brain, but whatever. It's how I freaking feel.

At least I can finally describe myself as melancholy. What a beautiful and poetic word for something so terrible.

Slater pulls away first. "Isla, come on."

"What?" I ask, face flushed.

"Please talk to someone."

"I'm fine."

He stares at me, but I avert my eyes because I can't hold his gaze. "You're not fine. I don't care who you talk to, whether me, or your parents, or a professional, or some stranger on the street, but *please* just talk to someone."

It's then that I realize that I'm not just hurting myself, I'm hurting him too. Because in my plummet to destruction, he's collateral damage. Tears leak from my eyes. "Gosh, I'm sorry." *I hate that I'm hurting you, but I can't seem to let you go. I'm sorry that I'm so selfish. I wish I could be anyone else. You deserve so much better.*

He wraps his arms around me and draws me close to his chest. Droplets of water land on my head.

With Raina gone, the lunch table feels extremely empty despite the influx of newcomers trying to shove their way into the limited space. Now I have no one else to talk to except Slater, and *everyone* is trying to talk to Slater.

I thought I felt excluded before, but now I *really* know what exclusion feels like. I can tell that Slater feels bad with the way he keeps looking over at me, but it's not his fault that I'm a loner.

On the other hand, I kind of like the fact that I'm not forced to talk. The only person I can talk to successfully these days is myself, and by talking, I mean criticizing.

I stab my fork on some gray looking chicken and the fork freaking breaks. *Ugh.* I don't bother getting a new one because I'm lazy, there's no chance I'm going to get my spot back, and the chicken doesn't look that appetizing anyway. With no food to focus my attention on, I listen to the lunch chatter.

"Are you guys going to the game tonight?" some guy named Carlos asks. People around the table perk up with excitement.

I furrow my eyebrows. The only sport that I know of is basketball, and basketball season is *definitely* over. Unless I'm some terrible girlfriend who has been keeping him from practice, which at this point, is also a possibility. I hope that's not the case though.

Slater looks at my plate of uneaten chicken. "Want to get food after school?" He asks, "We can get takeout and eat it in my car."

A frown cracks my face. I hate that he has to adjust his answer for me. "Sure, but don't you have a game to go to?"

"Nope."

"Oh, okay." *Hang out with your friends* is what I want to say, but I'm selfish. I think that has already been established. Instead, I ask, "Basketball season is over, right?"

He looks at my eyebrows and the grimace on my face, and laughs. It's one of the first real laughs that he has had this week. He used to laugh all the time. "Yeah, basketball season ended around the time of the formal. The game tonight is a soccer game."

"Cool." I don't know what else to do, so I squeeze his hand. He squeezes my hand back. The gesture is a thousand words and no words rolled into one.

Even my parents are noticing that something is off, and they're not observant at all. On my quest for a granola bar, my mom stares at me as I walk down the stairs and through the kitchen. Eventually, she blurts out, "What is wrong with you?"

My heart pounds against my rib cage, and my hands start to sweat. *Deflect, deflect, deflect.* "What are you even talking about, Mama? Are *you* okay?" It's basic gaslighting and I feel slightly bad, but it does the trick. My mom raises an eyebrow at me and settles for more staring.

Then my dad comes into the living room, takes a seat next to her, and they stare at me together. But it's not the staring that I have a problem with, it's the whispers that they think I can't hear.

I hear *everything*.

It's like I'm a caged animal whose only purpose in life is to provide entertainment. "What?" I ask. It comes out a little louder and angrier than I want it to.

"Don't speak to us like that. We're your parents," my dad says.

I want to go on a rant against filial piety, but instead I just let out a breath. "Sorry."

They don't address me, but they do continue staring. To make matters worse, I forgot about the granola bar.

In my room, I Google "how to feel better" on my laptop.

There's this article telling me to go outside, an instant no, and another one telling me to listen to music. With no other choice, I put on my earbuds and pull up some "girlboss" playlist, their words, not mine. Nothing changes. In fact, I can barely focus on the lyrics. In the end, I give up and slam my laptop shut.

When I look up, I see the daisies that Slater got for me and this feeling that I can't define intensifies. The crappy thing about this is that I have no tears left, so it all just boils up inside me.

Why can't this be a switch that I can simply turn off? Why does it have to ruin my life? Will I ever get better?

It's just so freaking cruel.

CHAPTER 19

It's a Wednesday when my principal, Dr. Richardson, calls my parents.

I almost don't believe it until my dad puts her on speaker phone.

"As I was saying Mr. Wu, will everyone be able to come in for a family meeting today? There are very important matters that we have to discuss." What? Today? I thought you had to schedule meetings weeks in advance to meet with the principal, but apparently, it's different with failing kids. We get special treatment.

"What is she saying?" Dad whispers to me.

"She wants us to come in for a meeting today. You're busy, right?" *Please be busy today, please be busy today, please be busy today.*

"We be there," my dad speaks into the phone. My heart drops, every single nerve in my body ignites, and my brain runs through every possible scenario. They're all bad.

"Great, does five work?" Dr. Richardson asks.

"Yes."

An hour later, I'm in a car with my confused parents.

"Are you getting an award?" my mom asks. "I can't wait to brag about this on WeChat. My daughter is getting an award from the principal herself."

I almost laugh. It's quite literally the exact opposite. "No."

My mom huffs. Just wait until the meeting, mom. It's all going to get *so* much worse.

"Well, did you do anything bad at school?" my mom continues. "If someone is bullying you, it's okay if you hit them in self-defense. I won't get mad and if the principal suspends you, we can start a petition."

"Yeah." My dad taps the wheel. Then my parents shoot each other a look. I know exactly what they're wondering... *Does this meeting have to do with my mood shift?*

I shrug. I want to hold off their wrath for as long as I can.

I let the principal tell them in her very chilly office. Dr. Richardson stands up to shake their hands. "Mr. Wu, Mrs. Huang, thanks for coming in."

"What happen?" my dad asks.

"Why don't you take a seat?" She smiles. She pushes to make room for her arms on the paraphernalia-filled desk before she starts speaking. All I can hear is my heart.

Thump.

Thump.

Thump.

"Isla failed all of her academic classes this semester." With that single sentence, my world tumbles.

My parents' jaws drop.

"Failed like F?" my mom whispers like she can't believe it. Like the thought never occurred in her mind.

"Yes. Now, it's not too late for her to salvage this, it's the first semester and we still have the second semester to go. I just wanted to call a meeting because this is very uncharacteristic of Isla according to her past records." Dr. Richardson looks at each of us. "Have there been any problems at home?"

That question again. They wouldn't understand if I told them the truth. If I told them that I feel numb and everything at the same time.

"No." My dad's nose is red, his eyebrows are furrowed into one line, and his mouth is twitching. I can just tell that all he wants to do is yell at me, and it's impressive how long he's kept his composure.

"Okay. Well, I highly recommend that Isla comes in for office hours *very* often and sees a therapist," Dr. Richardson's mouth continues moving, but I hear nothing else. My parents are staring out the window. They've stopped listening too.

The car ride back is silent, save for the noise of tires against the road and the occasional honk.

When we get home, my mom doesn't look at me, but asks, "Do you even want to go to college? There's no way you're getting into college now. You've ruined your future."

And then the house is silent too.

My second panic attack happens on a Saturday night.

This time there's no one to help me through it. I'm all alone, and I hate it.

Dr. Richardson's statement made the whole thing real. *Tangible.* Besides, my mom is right, I am futureless, and I have no one else to blame except myself. What am I going to do? What colleges are going to want a person who has failed a whole semester? Will my parents ever talk to me again?

A heavy weight sits on my heart, and the pain starts to suffocate me.

I keep my air intake at a rapid pace, but no oxygen fills my lungs. Eventually my face starts to tingle, my heart starts to palpitate, and the room starts to spin around me.

Then everything goes dark.

With my parents not talking to me, Slater is the only person in my life.

And because I'm afraid to be by myself, we're *constantly* together. Like even more than before. If we're not hanging out, we're on the phone, and if we're not on the phone, we're at school. I know that it's unhealthy, but I'm not strong enough to stop it.

Like an addict, I take another hit, no thoughts about how it will hurt the people around me until I come down from the high. I press call.

He answers on the third ring, voice groggy. "Hey."

"Hi."

"Car hangout?"

"Yeah."

"I'll be there in thirty."

We've repeated these lines so much that they have become a script.

He's never late, and today is not an exception. He is here in thirty, and he parks his car in the forested area that we've found to escape from my parents' view.

I reach out to kiss him, and when we're tired of kissing, there's silence. It's all so predictable.

His eyes are closed, and his mouth is fixed in a frown. I hate that I've reduced him to *this*.

So, I give him a piece of me. "I failed all of my classes this semester." It's barely a whisper, but he opens his eyes.

"You probably don't want to hear a sorry."

"Yeah."

He tucks a loose strand of hair behind my ear, and stares at me. "Oh, Isla. You forget that I have been through all of this. I know. I hate that this is happening to you."

"My parents won't talk to me anymore."

He sighs, and pulls my head against his chest. Like he's in pain too. Like he's in pain for me.

"I can't even cry anymore. How crappy is that?" I laugh self-deprecatingly.

"So crappy." I finally get a smile out of him. I resist the urge to take a picture and ruin the moment.

After a while, I whisper, "You're the center of my universe."

I expected a different reaction from him. A happy one.

Instead, his smile slips away.

A week later, Slater knocks on my door. My parents are at work so they don't see him. I don't know how they'd react if they knew that I was hanging out with my boyfriend instead of studying. Then again, maybe they wouldn't react at all. Sometimes, it feels like they've lost all hope for me.

"Hey, I didn't know we were going out today." I smile, clapping my hands in delight before wrapping my arms around his neck.

"We can't do this anymore."

What?

My hands fall back to my side. "What do you mean?" my voice cracks. I hate how weak I sound. "You can't break up with me, you're the only person I have left." Of course, the tears choose to come back now.

"I'm hurting you by enabling you to avoid your issues. I can't be the center of your universe. You have to be the center of your universe. When you place me above yourself, it only hurts us both." Tears fill his eyes.

"I didn't mean it. It was just something I said in the spur of the moment." *I did mean it.*

"I know for a fact that the last thing you need right now is me. I love you, I do, but for your own good, we just can't do this right now."

He told me he loved me for the first time and broke up with me in the same breath. *Impressive.*

"Okay." I shut the door on him. But it's the pain talking and acting on my behalf. Truthfully, I'm glad that I'm not dragging him down with me anymore. I wasn't strong enough to free him so I'm glad that he has freed himself. What I want to do is turn back, open the door, and shout, "I love you too, and I'm happy for you!"

But instead, I watch his car drive away in silence.

The following Monday is the worst.

I wake up with sore, bloodshot eyes from crying all night, and I don't even have time to eat breakfast. Then on the crowded morning train, I end up getting squished against the door.

However, at school is when everything truly goes to crap.

I once thought that the news of me and Slater's relationship was blown out of proportion, but the news of our breakup is even worse. I don't even know how they found out already. The whispers follow me down the hallway. All I can hear is my name getting repeated. *Over and over and over again.* I wish they were better at whispering.

In history, Lucy turns to me with a big smile. "I'm sorry to hear about you and Slater's breakup."

I sigh.

"But I'm not exactly surprised. I mean he was doing charity work, no offense."

I love how people say "no offense" and then their next words are totally offensive. "Okay, Lucy." I'm too tired to be angry, and she does kind of have a point.

"The only thing that I was surprised about was that he chose you in the first place."

I'm about to breathe out another "okay" before Elise interrupts me. "Gosh, Lucy, will you shut up for once in your life? Your jealousy radiates off you in waves."

"E, you can't talk to me like that. We're friends," Lucy frowns.

Elise rolls her eyes. "We were never friends."

Lucy's face drops, but she turns away to hide it. As mean as she can be, I feel bad for her. I know exactly what it feels like to crave Elise's approval.

Elise turns to me. "I'm sorry for everything. I was so jealous of you that I said and did some terrible things."

I can't muster any words so I pat her hand. Then she walks away, and I'm all alone again.

At lunch, I realize that I have nowhere to sit. I can't sit at my old table because it has been converted into the popular table and the only link that I had to the popular kids was through Slater, I can't sit with Raina because she definitely hates me now, and I definitely can't sit at a table by myself.

In the end, I choose the bathroom. Not the bathroom in front of the popular table, the bathroom on the second floor, in front of my math class. *Gosh, I'm such a high school loser cliché.*

Other than my toilet constantly trying to flush itself between bites of square pizza, I think I kind of like the bathroom stall. It's not suffocating like everywhere else, and I don't get judged.

The avoiding, the eating lunch in the bathroom, the sitting alone in classes, the standing around awkwardly in gym class becomes my new school routine before I realize it. The only continuity is that I still don't go to office hours.

CHAPTER 20

A month passes, and all of a sudden, it's my seventeenth birthday. This is the first year that none of my friends have posted a birthday post for me on social media. In fact, they don't acknowledge my birthday at all. But then again, I suppose I don't get to call them that anymore so they don't owe me *anything*.

The only birthday gift I do get is from Slater. The box sits on our kitchen table, like all other mail that my parents bring in, and I don't even realize that it's for me until I see the coffee-themed wrapping paper.

In the safety of my room, I unwrap the gift and a letter falls out. I set it aside for now and open the box. Nestled inside blue crinkle paper shreds, there's a copy of *Jane Eyre*, a gift card for a coffee shop, a large tub of mayo, and a Tiffany bracelet with a diamond in the middle.

Then I open the letter and read it in his voice.

Isla Wu,

Happy Birthday! You're 17! You probably opened the gift before you read this letter (we both know you're impatient, ha ha), but now I get to explain it. Most of the gift is probably pretty self-explanatory (i.e. a tub of mayo for your love for mayo, and a gift card so you can spill more coffee on me... joking, I promise), and now you finally have your own official copy of one of the greatest classics ever! I annotated in the margins so it'll kind of be like we're reading it together. I can't take credit for the bracelet, though. That was all my mom. Anyways, I miss you like crazy, and I'm rooting for you always. I know what you're going through sucks a ton, but if anyone can get through it, it's you. No doubts!

I love you,

Slater Wesbrook

A big, goofy grin plasters my face. It's my first real smile in weeks, and all I can think is how much I'll hate when it goes away.

Downstairs, I find my parents at the dinner table. With mouths etched in a line and eyes tracking my every movement, their expressions mirror each other.

"Come sit with us, Isla." That's the longest sentence my mom has said to me since the school meeting.

When I sit down, my dad starts talking. His words chase each other, and I can barely follow what he's saying. Then I hear, "We're putting you in therapy," and I fall against my chair.

I definitely heard wrong because my parents don't even believe in therapy. "What?"

"We're putting you in therapy," my dad repeats.

The second "What?" stems from shock. I don't even process that I'm saying it until after it comes out of my mouth.

"I think your baba said it perfectly clear. Both times," my mom says.

"Th-therapy?"

A minute of silence passes before my mom buries her face in her hands and starts crying. My mom never cries.

I start to cry, too. "Mama, Baba, I'm sorry that I failed. I'm sorry that I'll never be skinny, pretty, or smart enough. I wish more than anything that I could be the daughter that you deserve. I'm so sorry that I'm not."

That makes her cry harder. "I've pushed you too hard, and I've done all the wrong things. You've always been more than enough," she wipes her eyes. "I only said those things to motivate you to be the best that you can be. You understand why I did what I did, right?"

I don't answer her. I don't tell her that it's okay, because it's not. But some part of me does understand. Just a little bit.

"I'm sorry, Island." Apologizing is another thing that my mom never does. I guess it's a night of firsts.

"My name is actually Isla."

"Shhh. I'm your mama, and I am always right."

"I am too pushy about school, I'll admit it, but that's only because I don't want you to live the hard life that I did. But I will always be proud of you, no matter what happens. I'm sorry for making you think anything different." My dad looks sad.

These words are all I've ever wanted to hear from them – they're all I've ever craved – I only hate that it took them seventeen years to say it. But I'll take what I can get. "Thanks, Baba."

"You still need to get those grades up." Mom looks at me sternly.

"I will, I promise." And slowly, I start to believe that everything will turn out okay.

Besides, it's the first gift that my parents have ever gotten me on my birthday. That is, if therapy even counts as a gift. I'm going to ask them for a *real* present next year. Red envelopes on Chinese New Year aren't enough.

In the waiting room of the therapist's office, the walls are a light baby blue. It's the kind of color that coaxes you in and calms you, or at least according to the hippy dippy researchers of color psychology. I think I'm too anxious for it to work for me, though.

My parents have me squished in the middle of this already too small couch, and as if that wasn't enough, they're visibly nervous. My mom's eyes dart back and forth around the room, while my dad checks his watch and sighs every three seconds, like it's the therapist's fault that we arrived an hour early.

Watching them heightens my *own* anxiety, which makes my right leg bounce faster.

A lady with a black hijab and a bright smile walks up to me. "Isla Wu, right?"

"Yes, hi." My voice shakes with nerves.

"I'm Dr. Rashid. It's a pleasure to meet you." She turns her attention to my mom and dad. "And you must be her parents."

"Yes," my mom speaks for both of them.

"Lovely to meet you guys as well. Today is going to be pretty much an introductory session, and you guys are welcome to continue waiting here. There is a coffee machine and snacks by the front desk. If you need anything, please just ask Carmen." She points at the lady who checked us in.

"Thank you." My mom walks off with my dad toward the car. Of course, they're going out to do something fun while I'm stuck in therapy.

I glare at their backs.

Dr. Rashid motions for me to follow her into an office with an obnoxiously yellow couch filled with animal pillows. "Please, make yourself comfortable. As you may see, I love animal pillows." Her laugh is a sort of tinkling sound that reminds me of a fairy.

"I understand that you're here because you've been feeling down."

I guess that's one way you could describe it.

"Yeah." I nod, crossing and uncrossing my legs.

"How long have you been feeling this way?"

"Since thirteen, but it's been extra intense this time around. I used to be able to handle it."

Dr. Rashid has a pretty good listening face. It's exactly what it's supposed to look like. Slightly creased eyebrows, eye contact, a head that nods every few seconds. However, I'm socially awkward so I avoid her gaze and look down at my palms for a second.

"How are things right now?"

"Terrible."

Dr. Rashid continues nodding her head, urging me to continue.

"I've lost all motivation. I'm failing all of my classes at school, my friends have all abandoned me, I lost the sweetest boy in the world because he couldn't deal with my self-destruction, and I'm pretty sure my parents hate me." I bite my lip to keep my tears from escaping. It doesn't work. "I really wish I could get better because everything in my life would change if I did."

"It sounds like you're putting quite a lot of pressure on yourself to get better." She hands me a box of tissues. "From what I've heard, you're feeling a sense of isolation?"

"I mean I guess you could say that. The thing is that I don't know how to feel. I guess, objectively speaking, I have my parents, but they're not the easiest people to talk to on the planet and they don't understand what I'm going through at all."

"Are you trying to hide your emotions from them?"

"A little bit. Everything that's happening to me only causes them pain so I try to put on a brave face for them."

By the end of the session, I've gone through half the box of tissues, but I do feel better. It's like a little weight has been lifted off my chest.

I go to therapy every Wednesday afternoon. I think I've even started looking forward to my sessions. Dr. Rashid is the first person I've ever talked to about *all* of my emotions, and she lets me rant about my day and she has also been encouraging me to take step-by-step actions to re-normalize my life. Only a month after my first therapy session do I make the first step, but I won't blame myself because I'm supposed to be cutting myself some slack.

It's like pulling a trigger when I finally gather the nerve to talk to Raina in precalculus.

"Hey." I'm scared that she doesn't hear me for a second, and I'll definitely lose my nerve if I have to repeat anything.

But then Raina whispers "hi" back to me and my breathing goes back to normal.

"I'm sorry."

"It's okay. I know you were going through hell. I'm sorry I wasn't more understanding and didn't even texting you on your birthday."

Before I'm able to say anything else, Mr. Walter starts lecturing. *Hey, I have to get my grades up!*

But we do continue speaking on our way to the cafeteria.

"I've missed you so much." She hugs me in the lunch line and I hug her back with tears in my eyes. We're surrounded by other chattering people, but it still feels like we're the only ones here.

"I've missed you too. So much." I pat her arms.

"Where have you been? I never saw you in the cafeteria."

"That's a story for another time." I laugh as I grab a burger. Regardless, I don't regret the time I spent eating in a toilet stall. Because of it, I've kind of learned to embrace loneliness.

She turns to pout at me while we try to find a place to sit in the crowded cafeteria. *Gosh, I haven't been here in a while.*

Eventually, Raina guides me to a table in the middle of the cafeteria where three girls and two guys are already sitting. It's far away from the table we used to sit at and Elise and Aisha's table.

"Gail, Yeona, Selene, Ben, Bryan, meet my best friend, Isla." She beams. It's kind of crazy how big our school is because I have never met any of these people in my life.

"Hi." I wave.

A red-haired girl with sparkly eyeshadow speaks up first. "Nice to meet you, my real name is Abigail, but everyone calls me Gail."

"Hi. Thanks." My face flusters instantly. I should've said "Nice to meet you too" or something remotely normal.

Thankfully, Raina swoops in. "Gail recruited me to math club and then all of us just started hanging out." Of course, Raina is smart enough to get freaking recruited to the math club.

"Oh, that's fun." I don't know why I'm so awkward.

"Yeah. The B squared aren't nerds like the rest of us, though." Raina turns to me, hides her mouth with one hand, and whispers loudly as she points to the two guys with her other hand, "They're theater geeks."

"I'd rather be a theater geek than a nerd," a guy with waves and painted fingernails shoots back.

The other boy with curly hair and glasses wraps his shoulder around him and pecks his temple. "Yeah, me and Ben are cooler than all of you guys."

"Lies.," Gail's eyes are lingering on Raina.

"Just because we're dating doesn't mean you guys need to gang up on us," Bryan says.

Raina groans. "You always use the dating excuse. You're the ones claiming that you're cooler than us."

"You tell her, Rainie." Gail laughs, reaching towards Raina for a high five. I can't help but frown. Despite knowing Raina for years, we never had nicknames for each other. There's now also a part of Raina that I'll never know. That only they know. *Rainie.*

"Well, I'm Selene, the string of the group," a girl with curly dark brown ringlets changes the subject. "Well-rounded. Mathlete and theater geek. Best of both worlds."

The last girl tosses her shiny black hair back and laughs. "I'm Yeona."

Raina turns to me. "So, this is the group. B squared is actually taking us to see a musical this Saturday and then we're going to get Korean barbecue at Yeona's parents' restaurant. Want to join?"

I look at the table to observe everyone else's reactions.

"Yeah, come with us!" Selene gives me a big smile.

The others have blank looks on their faces. I might be socially awkward, but I know when I'm not wanted. "Sorry, I have something to do, but next time, yeah?"

Raina frowns at me for a second, but then the chatter continues and I see how well she fits in. I don't think she's ever seen her this comfortable, even in our old friend group. Of course, I'm a little jealous that she's moved on without me, but she seems happy and for that, I'm happy. *I swear.*

On Thursday, Elise, Aisha, and I are at the lockers at the same time.

"Hey, guys." Elise and Aisha are in the middle of their conversation when I interrupt them.

They wear matching expressions of shock on their faces, and I can't help but wonder how it all came to this? How did two of my closest friends become strangers in a matter of seconds?

"Hi," Elise says first while Aisha just smiles at me. Her infomercial smile. I've missed it.

"Elise, I just wanted to apologize for going after a guy that I know you liked and not telling you the truth about my feelings," I word vomit.

"No, I should be the one that's sorry. I was so," Elise's voice cracks, "awful to you. I threw this beautiful friendship away for a guy that never liked me. He always liked you, and everyone knew that. I should've just accepted it instead of being a hateful brat. I'm so sorry, Isla."

I pull her in for a hug, and Aisha wraps her arms around us.

After a minute of silence, Elise asks, "Do you think we'll ever be as close as we were?"

"No," I answer truthfully. Elise and our history together will always be a part of me, but I don't think I can be close friends with someone who uses my insecurities against me. I know that it was a mistake, and maybe I'm unforgiving for this, but I just can't. It hurts too much.

Elise nods and quickly turns her eyes away from me. It hurts me that I'm hurting her, but I just can't. Not now.

"How was your seventeenth birthday?" Aisha asks.

"We weren't sure what to do because we thought you'd want your space after everything," Elise explains.

"It was good." I smile. "I finally got a copy of *Jane Eyre*." I don't tell them who it was from because some things are sacred.

"Finally!" Aisha exclaims. "I'm so glad you won't be able to send us screenshots of quotes anymore."

"Yeah, I'll be sending you the actual pictures of the quotes now. Get ready for multiple angled, different filtered shots of 'I am no bird and no net ensnares me.'"

Aisha groans, and then we look at each other and burst out laughing.

Friendships happen and fade away, but I am grateful that I got to experience ours. The memories will stay with me forever, but now it's time for a new chapter. One where I choose myself.

CHAPTER 21

Eventually, I start to learn to choose myself.

Outside my window, the sky changes from light to dark. Before I know it, the clock reads ten and I'm still studying for this math test.

"Go to sleep," my mind's whispers.

"What if I didn't study enough?" I ask myself.

"Go to sleep."

Months earlier, I probably would've refused to listen and argued back, but this time I do. Listen, I mean.

I don't want sleep to be this unicorn that I keep chasing but can never find. I think that I deserve to finally capture it. Because what is life if you're not reaping the benefits and letting something as fickle as grades consume you?

When I put my head on the pillow, it's lights out instantly, and the next morning, the only thing on my mind is the fact that I got eight hours of sleep. Plus, the math test was actually kind of fun.

Now, I'm in math once again, waiting for the results of my new approach. I'm way more nervous than I should be, and my heart skips a beat every time Mr. Walker stomps near me. After what seems like forever, he drops a test on my desk. My hands shake while I pick it up. Then I turn the test over so quickly that it falls on the floor, adding another step to my dilemma.

Then finally, I see my grade. It's a B.

Tears exude from my eyes, one after another in a single file line, and my mouth cracks into a smile. I don't know if anyone notices that I'm sobbing in the back of the math classroom because I'm so hyper focused on this grade, but I don't really care.

It's the highest math test score that I've had in ages. My parents definitely won't be happy, but I'm happy. Like jump out of my seat, dance around, kind of happy.

Raina congratulates me.

I'd be lying if I said that my mood doesn't dampen a little when I see her perfect grade. However, this time, I don't let it show. I refuse to punish her again for my own insecurities. "Thanks, Raina."

It is still the best news that I've had in weeks. I really *needed* this.

When I'm finally in my room after school, I find myself with Slater withdrawal.

I wish more than anything to talk to him so I turn to the next best thing, *Jane Eyre*.

His annotations are in black ink and reading the book with them makes me feel like he's right next to me. I annotate under his annotations and it's kind of like we're conversing with each other.

Rochester is a big simp. But I guess I kind of understand.

I burst out laughing and write under his neat scrawl, *Yeah, me too.*

I read the book to the end and don't go to sleep until four in the night.

"Dr. Rashid!" I beam as I open the door to her office.

"Hey, Isla," she looks pleased to see me happy. "How are you feeling today?"

"Terrific. I reconciled with Aisha, Elise, and Raina, and I made an okay grade on my math test."

"You go girl!" Dr. Rashid high fives me.

"Thanks. I don't know why, but I still feel so much envy. I just can't feel happy for others that are better than me. How do I not feel like this anymore?"

"That's a good question, Isla. Why do you feel that people are better than you?" she clicks her pen and opens her note pad.

I shrug. "Like some people make better grades than me and subconsciously, I label them as better than me. For example, my best friend, Raina. She makes great grades and even though I love her to pieces, I get so jealous. That's why I couldn't talk to her for a while. I couldn't handle that she was acing everything while I was failing."

Dr. Rashid nods, but before she can say anything, I cut her off.

"And guess what? She has cool new friends now and they want nothing to do with me. Now she's probably going to force me to eat lunch with them too because I have nowhere left to go, and I'm just going to feel even more isolated and jealous." I pause to breathe. In the heat of the moment, I almost forget that oxygen is necessary. "I'm sorry that was super long and you probably think so much less of me now."

"Don't apologize for your emotions. Be proud that you can admit them. We all get jealous. Objectively, jealousy stems from a feeling of lack. It doesn't mean that you're not enough, despite how much it may feel that way. Just remember to celebrate your successes."

"Dr. Rashid, that is so cliché." I laugh. "How am I supposed to focus on my own successes when I have none? The most successful thing that I've done this week was not fail my math test."

"Isla, dear, don't discredit yourself. You've put in hard work and effort and now you're succeeding. Think of what past you would say. Besides, look at you, just seventeen years old with the strength to acknowledge how you feel and seek help. There are people way beyond your years that still don't know how to do that."

"That's not going to help get me into college. On the other hand, people with good grades will get into elite schools."

"College admissions looks at you overall, not just your grades. And so, what if you don't get into a top college? Ten years from now, will that matter?"

"Yes. My parents will be so mad if I don't get into a good college after how much they've sacrificed for me."

"But how will *you* feel?"

"I don't know." I really don't, but I think I feel semi-comfortable in the unknown.

For now, at least. Hey, I'm only a junior!

"Mama, I didn't like that you basically called me *pàng* today."

"What do you mean? I never said that." My mom looks up from her breakfast of eggs covered in soy sauce to stare. My dad stares at me too.

"Yes, you did. The first thing that you told me this morning was 'your face looks like a *bao*' while laughing and shaking your head."

"I was making an observation. Can I not make observations anymore?"

"Your observation made me feel really bad about myself."

"Okay, Isla. I will take that into account and rethink things that might make you feel sensitive."

In the name of getting better, my parents and I have decided to hold each other accountable for the hurtful things that we say. I wish it was working out perfectly, but it's not. It's passive aggressive with a touch of gaslighting, but we're *trying*.

"Okay." I don't know what else to say. No one ever tells you how uncomfortable it is to call your parents out.

"Okay." She waves at the table. "Sit down and eat. I already filled your plate."

This is what both confuses and reassures me the most. The fact that she says such mean things, but does kind gestures while playing them off nonchalantly. "Thanks."

She just stares at me, telepathically pressuring me to take my first bite. When I do, she asks, "What do you think?"

"It's delicious. You know that I love eggs."

She nods but doesn't say anything else.

On the other hand, my dad has been taking a more active approach. Dr. Rashid has definitely been talking to my parents because now my dad tries to give me daily positive encouragement. Today's is a "You can do it."

"Do what, Baba?"

"Whatever you need to do today." He smiles and straightens his back. He's oddly self-satisfied–like he knows something that I don't.

"Oh, okay. Thanks?"

He vigorously nods his head up and down.

I raise my eyebrow at him, but I would be lying if I said I didn't appreciate the efforts that they have been making. In fact, it's sort of their profession of love for me and their guarantee that no matter what happens, they'll always be rooting for me.

It's the first time that I have been to Raina's house since winter formal and it just feels weird.

Raina and I are sitting on her white rug, but there's no Elise and Aisha. Their spots are left untouched and I can't help but look up every few minutes, searching for them. But they aren't here, and there's a chance they'll never be here again.

I'm also slightly surprised but thankful that she didn't invite her new friends. I don't think I can handle sitting in awkward silence while everyone else is having fun. I already do that for forty-five minutes too much during lunch every day.

Raina looks at me. "How are you? Seriously."

"I'm okay, I think." I let out a breath, trying to ease the tension inside me. "Truly, everything is going better and I'm in a way better mindset, but I think it's going to take a little more time until I feel great."

Raina hugs me. "I'm so happy for you."

"Thanks, Raina."

Raina's eyebrows are furrowed as she stares at me, opening and closing her mouth repeatedly.

"Ask me." I laugh.

"WhathappenedtoyouandSlater?" She throws it out as one word.

"Can you repeat that?" I cup my ear. Yeah, I totally understood her.

Raina tucks a lock of hair behind her ear and a dimple appears underneath her mouth. "What happened to you and Slater?"

"Nothing bad, I promise. It just got to the point where I was putting him on this pedestal and hurting both of us."

"Oh."

"I do miss him like crazy." I pause. "I'm in love with him."

Raina smiles self-assuredly. "I knew it."

"I know, I know.," I laugh. "I can't even pinpoint the exact moment. I just knew and I was scared to admit it to myself. I guess it's too late now."

"Girl, what are you talking about? It's not too late."

I smile sadly. "I really did a number on him, Raina. I dragged him into some crap and he was too nice to even complain. I only wish I fell apart later so we could've had happiness longer."

Raina is silent for a minute. "You know he stares at you during lunch, right?"

"What are you talking about?"

"You may not notice, but I have a clear view of him from my seat. He looks at you a lot, Isla. It's all wistful and very puppy dog."

"You're kidding," I shake my head in disbelief.

Raina shakes her head. "From what I can see, he still loves you too and he's just waiting for you to reach out because he wants everything to be on your timing."

"He is a really good guy, isn't he?"

She nods. "Do you think you're in the right mindset to be with him?"

I let her words sink in before I speak again. "Yeah, I think I'm ready."

"So, what are you waiting for? Text him."

I stare at my phone, my heart starts to beat uncontrollably, and my fingers shake as I text him for the first time in months.

Me: *Hey*

Then I cover my face and throw my phone across her room. "Gosh, I cannot believe you just made me do that."

"You're welcome," Raina sings.

I jokingly glare at her but from the corner of my eye, I'm staring at my phone. Raina notices and leans forward to squeeze me, placing her chin on my shoulder. We both stare at my phone together.

"Do you love Mark?" I ask.

"You're trying to distract yourself." Raina laughs.

I pout and give her my best puppy eyes.

She sighs. "No, I don't think so. Don't get me wrong, he's a great first, but it's not all consuming like the way that I imagine love is."

"In my opinion, only toxic love is all consuming."

"You know what I mean. There are no sparks, no excitement, and I really want all of that."

"You're not going to feel like that forever. You're going to want comfort and stability." I try to reassure her.

"Yeah, but I just don't like him like him, you know? I see him more as a friend."

"Will you break up with him?"

"I don't know. It's just so easy."

I nod. I don't understand, but I understand at the same time. Before I can say anything though, my phone pings. Me and Raina race towards it together.

Slater: *Hey, you.*

Jumping up and down and hugging my phone to my chest, I squeal, "He said hi back!" I know now that I don't need him but I *really* want him.

Raina jumps with me. "You better not break up this time or I'll stop believing in love," she jokingly warns me.

"Nothing is certain. He only said hi back."

"It's a start." Raina grins.

Slater: *I miss you.*

I don't tell Raina this time, but she is right. This is a start.

CHAPTER 22

"Slater and I are going out this Saturday."

"Are you excited?" Dr. Rashid asks.

"I'm super excited. It still feels like a freaking dream. I've missed him so much."

"Well, I'm happy for you, Isla and proud of the effort that you've put in."

"Thanks, Dr. Rashid. I have a question for you."

Dr. Rashid nods at me.

"Even before the breakdown, I used to get these random spurts of numbness. What did they mean and how do I make sure that I don't get them anymore?"

"That's a good question, Isla. What do you think they meant?"

I jokingly frown. "Come on, Dr. Rashid. You're the therapist with the fancy degree."

"Come on, Isla. You're the high school student."

"Fine, I think the numbness stemmed from both this sort of out of place feeling and unmanageable stress. In order to cope, I just shut down from emotional exhaustion. I guess I can try to prevent them by being more conscious of my emotions and dealing with them instead of trying to hide them."

"Good, Isla." Her beaming smile reflects her pride in my growth.

And just like that, I finally understand what I felt. Or maybe I understood all along but pretended to not understand because I didn't want to deal with it.

His car is parked out in front of my house for the first time in months. I almost can't believe my eyes.

Both of my parents look over my shoulder.

"Is that Slater?" my mom asks.

"Yeah, we're going out today. Is that okay?" In my excitement, I just remembered that I forgot to ask my parents. Oops.

My mom nods, my dad says, "Seize the day." I think it's his motivation of the day. I practically trip over myself running out of the house.

"Hi!" I get in his car and close the door.

His smile stretches his face. "I missed you, Isla Wu."

"I missed you, too, Slater Wesbrook."

His smile grows even wider.

"Thanks for the birthday gift. It meant a lot."

"Of course. You mean a lot to me."

My heart does jumping jacks in my chest. In the spur of the moment, I almost forget to hand him the *Jane Eyre* book.

Slater raises an eyebrow at me, but takes the book anyway.

"This isn't for you to keep, of course. You have to return it back to me once you finish but I just thought that you'd like reading the book with my annotations too."

"You're so right. Thank you."

"No, thank you. The book was my anchor to you and I just read your annotations when I missed you. I'm sorry that I hurt you and I love you." I slap my hands over my mouth. I wanted the words to come out somewhat romantically. Not in the freaking car in the middle of an apology.

"It's okay, and I love you, too." He looks right at me. "And as much as I'd love to kiss you right now, I can't because your dad is burning holes through me with his eyes."

"Hit the pedal, Wesbrook." My grin is unstoppable.

We find ourselves at the only bakery in my neighborhood. The one whose coffee I spilt on Slater the first time we met.

The bells tell me they miss me, don't ask me how I know, I just know. The same mustached man is working at the counter, but unlike the bells, I doubt he recognizes me. Regardless, it's kind of a full circle moment.

Slater holds my hand as we wait for the guy to notice us. I can't stop staring at Slater, afraid that he might just dissipate into thin air.

"What do you all want?" mustached man asks.

"Caramel cold brew and a chicken biscuit with a side of mayo." I smile.

"Just a regular iced coffee, please."

I turn to Slater. "I'm paying and you can't do anything about it. Also, your coffee order is lame."

He mock gasps. "She's bossy and mean."

"Suck it up." I laugh. My mouth hurts from smiling so much, but I can't stop. It's Slater Wesbrook and he is here. Standing right next to me. He looks at me and starts laughing too. Nothing is funny. From the corner of my eye, I can see mustached man roll his eyes at us.

"You know, this is the first time I've been here since the first day of school."

"Wait, why?" I stare at him until slowly, the realization falls over his face and he starts to laugh. "This place?"

"Yeah."

"Well, we can recreate it. You can spill your coffee again and I won't mind. In fact, I'd probably thank you." He winks at me.

"You forget that that was one of the most embarrassing moments I've ever had in my life."

"It was one of the best moments of my life."

My heart flutters inside my chest, but I try to play it off. "I'm not wasting expensive coffee."

"Next time, then. I mean, the third time's the charm, after all."

I giggle but I don't give him an answer. *Absolutely no way.*

Mustached man places our order on the counter and then we just walk around the forested streets of my neighborhood.

"How is therapy going?" Slater asks.

"Really good, actually. My therapist is pretty great and I think all the sessions are actually helping me. I really didn't expect them to."

"That's amazing, Isla."

"Thanks. For everything, you know? If it wasn't for you, I don't think I'd be taking therapy seriously."

He stops in the middle of the street to wrap his arms around me. "I'm so proud of you," he whispers into the top of my head. I've been getting that phrase a lot these days but its luster still hasn't worn off. I've never thought I could be someone that people could just be proud of.

I smile and squeeze my arms around him. I never understood how much I could miss his hugs until they were gone.

When we're walking in silence again, I gather the nerve to ask, "Do you think you've healed from her death?"

Before, I was too preoccupied with myself to notice the emotional scars that mar him, but now I do. I see them as glaring manifestations in his behavior, how he's always making sure that the people around him are smiling, how close of a relationship he has with his parents, how much he cares. *I see it all now.*

"I don't think I will ever get over it completely, but yeah. I think I'm healed. I wish that I was a better brother to her when she was alive."

I squeeze his hand.

"You know, I went through something extremely similar to you when I first lost her. I was sad for a very, very long time and searching for places to put my self-worth in.," He takes a breath. "In fact, that's actually how I knew I had to let you go. I knew that you were slowly starting to put your self-worth in me and if I continued letting you do that, I would've become an inhibitor to your progress."

"You were right."

"I didn't want to be. Trust me, it was so difficult to let you go but I knew that this was the only way you could get better."

I lay my head on his shoulder and sigh. "I always find myself in awe of you, Slater Wesbrook."

"Right back at you, Isla Wu." He lays his head on top of my head.

This time is going to be different. This time there's not going to be an art project, jealous friends, or suffocating, overthinking thoughts. This time it's going to be just *us.*

Thursday is the first time in months that I don't wake up and inspect my body in the mirror. I almost don't realize it until I walk out the door.

It's a good feeling that leaves me thinking maybe, just maybe, I've been too harsh on myself. Maybe I don't have to see the beauty standard as the models with flat stomachs and long legs. Maybe I'm *beautiful* with all the softness, the big thighs, and the bloated stomach.

Just maybe.

On the subway, a pretty girl sits in front of me and I feel ashamed for thinking that I was pretty, too, because I'm not *that* pretty. But, then again, maybe beauty doesn't need to be measured through comparison to others. At least that's what the inspirational quotes tell you.

But maybe they are right. Maybe she's pretty, but maybe I'm pretty too.

Maybe. Maybe. *Maybe.*

I get to my AP Literature class on time and take my seat next to Raina.

"Hey." She looks glad to see me.

"Hi."

"I heard that Mrs. Robins is passing our graded essays back at the end of class."

I groan. "Seriously?"

"Yeah."

"I hate when teachers do that. Why can't they just pass it out first so we can get it over with?"

"Apparently it will distract us from her teaching."

I roll my eyes. "Not getting the essay back first is what will distract me from her teaching."

Slater pulls out the seat next to me. "What are we talking about?"

"Mrs. Robins giving us our essays back at the end of class," Raina says.

Slater frowns. "That sucks."

I turn to face him. "What are you doing here?"

"I'm in this class. It's been like what, eight months? I'm surprised that you still haven't noticed and honestly, a little hurt." The corner of his mouth lifts up.

I lightly punch his shoulder. "You know what I mean. There are assigned seats and you just stole Brent's."

"Well, I told Mrs. Robins that I can't really see from the back and she was happy to let me choose a seat that would suit my bad eyesight better."

"You have perfect vision and even if you didn't, we're halfway through the year."

Slater puts a finger over his lips and winks.

I whistle. "Well, color me impressed, Wesbrook. Your deceit knows no bounds."

He laughs and when Brent gets to class a minute before the bell rings, Slater tells him, "Your new seat is in the back." It's a brisk, to the point statement, the rudest that Slater can possibly be, and it warms my heart. I can't help but beam at him.

And true to her word, Mrs. Robins spends the whole time teaching about satire and hands back our papers in the last three minutes of class.

It's a ninety. My first A since forever. It also gives me the courage to check my grades in the online gradebook.

Once the freaking slow app loads, I find out that my grades are all B's, ranging from a low B in math to mid Bs in all the other subjects.

"Are you checking your grades?" Raina asks.

"Yeah. I have all Bs!"

"Wow, congrats!"

"I'm so in awe of you, Isla Wu." Slater squeezes my hand.

"Thanks guys." My smile stretches across my face and I can feel the joy take root, seeping over every centimeter of my body. It's kind of funny that once I would've cried over these grades, but now, I'm ecstatic.

CHAPTER 23

I once wanted to be like the ocean, but I think that's changed now.

Because I will never be like the ocean. I won't ever be fearless and perfect and indomitable. There will be days where I overthink and cry over miniscule situations, and sometimes fear will overpower me.

But that's okay, because I will be Isla Wu. And Isla Wu does not do heights, no matter how many times that Slater Wesbrook claims it will be fun.

"No." I firmly shake my head. We're at Coney Island again, but this time it's not snowing and we've stumbled onto the boardwalk. And by stumbled, I mean the first thing we did upon exiting the train station, Slater insisted that parking was going to be hard to find, was head for the roller coasters. And by we, I mean Slater.

"It will be fun." He pouts again. "Look, the roller coaster's name is Cyclone."

"That does not make me feel any better."

"It's been open since the 1920s, so it's a piece of history?"

"I'm feeling worse."

He kisses me.

"Slightly better."

Slater laughs. "But in the name of fear-overcoming, we should ride the roller coaster."

"Technically, we already rode a roller coaster for our fear project and my fear is still here."

"What? What do you mean the fear project hasn't worked?" The corner of his mouth lifts into a smile.

"So, you mean to tell me that school doesn't actually apply to real life?" I add.

He mock gasps. "Now that is just a travesty."

When the laughter fades, I look at him and then the roller coaster again. "Fine, let's do it." Maybe the adrenaline rush will help soothe my school stress.

"Are you sure?"

"Weren't you trying to convince me?"

"Yeah, but I don't want to force you into anything."

"Slater, I pinky promise that I made this decision on my own. Though I will probably regret it though.

He wears a big smile as he picks me up and spins me around.

When we get off the ride, I'm reminded once again that I will never not be afraid of roller coasters. But I'm a happy camper because Slater held onto my hand the entire ride.

We walk alongside the waves with shoes in our hands. Halfway through our stroll, a wave of gray water combined with a dirty diaper almost crashes into me.

I love it here.

"Isla!" Raina calls after me in the crowded hallway.

"Hey." I raise my eyebrow. "What's going on?"

Raina takes my hand and drags me into a quiet corner.

"Just so you know, I still have to get stuff from my locker." I chuckle.

"Gail asked me out," Raina confesses.

"Oh, my gosh!" I'm not surprised. The signs were sort of obvious—even to me.

"I know."

"What about Mark?"

Raina sinks down the brick siding and buries her face in her hands. "I don't know. Everything is so complicated."

"At least you have great grades." I'm surprised to find that there's no malice behind my statement. It's a simple declaration of fact.

Raina mumbles something that I can't hear. I don't think I've ever seen her *this* affected, and it weirds me out a little bit. She's steady Raina. And I don't know what to do because I've never had to play her part. I settle for more questions. "Do you still see him as just a friend?"

Raina nods.

"Oh." I'm at a loss for words. If our roles were switched, Raina would probably give me her brash, brutal opinion, so I try to channel her. "You should break up with him."

Raina sighs. "I know. But he's such a great guy and I wouldn't even know how to go about it. I still want to be friends with him."

I don't know either. It's times like these that makes me wish that Aisha and Elise were still fixtures in our lives. They would have multi step approaches for every miniscule detail. All I can do is croak out a weak, "Just do it. You're going to regret it if you don't."

"You're right. Thanks."

A beat passes before I fire my next question. "Do you like her?"

Raina doesn't speak for a bit, but when she does, it's a whisper. "I don't know."

"And that's perfectly fine." I squeeze her shoulder. "Thanks for asking me for advice."

"Well, obviously. Who else would I ask?"

I look at the hallway to avoid looking into her eyes. "It's just," I murmur, the words hanging in the air like a weight. My chest tightens, like I'm trying to hold everything in, but it's bursting to spill out. "You have so many new friends now and our relationship has always been you giving and me taking. Sorry."

Raina pulls me into a tight hug. "Isla, you are my person and no one can replace you. I love that I'm your support system and that you're mine too."

I beam at her.

Later, in the school bathroom, I hear stifled sobs from the middle stall. I shift my balance between my feet and I try to put myself in that person's shoes. Would I rather someone give me privacy or actually care and ask me what's wrong? I mean, there's a bathroom that I could go to downstairs.

The tiny voice in my brain chooses the latter.

I fidget with my nails for another minute before calling out, "Hey, are you okay?"

Shuffles reverberate from the stall. "I'm fine, go away."

I know exactly whose voice it is. *Lucy.*

"Hey, it's Isla. I'm serious. Are you okay?"

She huffs and stays quiet. I give up and head for the door, but that's when she softly says, "No."

"Do you want to talk about it?"

It's more silence before another hesitant, "Yeah."

"Okay."

"Okay. But I'm going to stay in the stall to prevent more humiliation."

I laugh. "Believe it or not, I used to sit and eat lunch in the bathroom."

"Of course, you did." She pauses. "Sorry, that was mean, wasn't it?"

"It's fine." And surprisingly, it was.

"Well, I failed a test."

"Been there, done that." I hope I sound sympathetic, not mean.

"And I basically have no real friends so my life is pretty great."

"I'm sorry." Lucy might've been awful to me, but I do feel bad. No one deserves that.

She laughs pitifully. "It's like I keep sucking up to these people and making them my world, but in the end, all they do is end up hating me. I guess I have a repulsive personality."

"Or maybe you're befriending the wrong people."

"You know, at this point, I don't even care about having friends. My parents are definitely going to kill me when they see my grades."

"Speaking from someone who has been through what you're going through, don't worry. They're more understanding than you'd think."

"You say that, but you don't know my parents."

"I guess I don't, but I think that on the inside, our parents really just want what's best for us."

She huffs and there's a moment of silence before she speaks again. "What was it like? Going through your... um—"

"Breakdown?"

"Yeah."

"It was terrible, but now I'm in a much better state mentally than I've ever been so I guess, in a twisted way, that I'm grateful for it. I have all Bs now."

"Huh." I know that she doesn't mean to sound condescending, but to someone like Lucy and past me, Bs are fails. I'm just glad that I don't have this mentality anymore. This competitive battlefield of a high school can ruin your mental health and self-perception if you let it.

"And guess what, my Bs are perfect. I'm proud of them because they're a measure of my resilience and that's what grades should be. One bad grade will not ruin your life, I promise." I can't believe these words are flowing through my mouth, and I also can't believe that I agree with them wholly.

"Thanks. That made me feel a lot better," Lucy says. "Seriously."

"Yeah, of course. Well, I guess I will see you in history?"

"Yeah."

Before I can fully open the bathroom door, I hear Lucy call out. "Hey, Isla?"

"Yeah?"

"I'm really sorry for everything."

"I forgive you." With a grin on my face, I realize in my next class that I still very much have to use the restroom.

I plop onto the familiar couch and curl up in a fetal position.

"Good afternoon, Isla." Dr. Rashid smiles.

"Sorry, I'm just so tired. I barely got any sleep last night because I was up binging an entire season of *Gilmore Girls*. I also feel slightly guilty because I could've used this time to study."

"Everyone needs a moment of reprieve once in a while."

"You're so right. Guess what."

Dr. Rashid plays along. "What?"

"I don't feel that fostering of jealousy toward Raina anymore. I actually feel happy that she's happy and succeeding," I pause. "But that might just be because I'm happy since I have Slater and okay grades again."

"Isla, what did I tell you about discrediting yourself?"

"Don't." I tuck a piece of hair behind my ear and frown.

"Exactly. This is progress. Be proud of yourself."

I nod and sigh once again. "That's such a difficult thing to do."

"I know, but you will get the hang of it, and then one day, it will just come naturally. As natural as breathing."

I nod again. "Dr. Rashid, I see everything now."

"What do you mean by that?"

"It's just that I used to be so preoccupied with myself and thinking that I was the only one struggling, but now I realize how everyone else is too."

Dr. Rashid nods with a smile.

"It's so invalidating when no one talks about their struggles because we could totally help each other out if we did," I pause. "I want to do something about it."

"Then do it."

CHAPTER 24

There's a super flowery scent in the air, that might be the heavily perfumed stranger walking past me, and the sun is so, so bright when I exit the rusty subway station. It's a weird day for the wintery February.

And even weirder, I feel a new burst of confidence embrace me as I go through my mental checklist of items. I see my first one leaning against his locker, chatting with his friends. He's so effortlessly cool.

"Hey." I tap his shoulder.

"Isla." He wraps his arms around me, despite the fact that his friends are watching and making fun of him. For the first time, I don't care.

"Ready to go?"

"Yeah." He smiles. "My girlfriend is a champ!"

My face flushes crimson red. "It's not like that."

"Yeah, it is," he looks at me and mouths, "My activist."

We enter a classroom full of students and I can't suppress the smile that stretches my face. Slater walks to the back of the classroom, leaving me in front of everybody.

With support from my therapist and my favorite people, I started my own club at school. It's sort of a weird hybrid club with a simultaneous focus on sharing our mental health issues and culture appreciation, and honestly, I was surprised when the school approved it. And I was even more surprised to see the number of people on the signup sheet.

Today is the first meeting and my hands shake as I stare at all these people who are here for *my* club. I have to remind myself that most of them probably just came for the free donuts to calm my nerves. Slater and Raina shoot me encouraging looks and I even see Lindsay from my gym class.

People are still socializing and I'm too nervous to talk in front of everyone right now, so I walk over to Lindsay. "Hey, welcome! It's so good to see you here."

"Me, too. I'm so proud of you." She reaches to hug me. "And I miss you in gym. I wish gym was a two-semester requirement for upperclassmen too."

"I miss you, too, but I definitely don't. I'm thankful that gym was only one semester for me. One semester too much." I laugh. "How is it, though? Is Coach Crosby still a misogynistic butthole?" Gym class sort of feels like a lifetime away.

"Yeah, but I kind of called him out on it so he's at least aware. He is trying harder to not be a misogynistic butthole, but sometimes it slips."

I reach for a high five. "Lindsay, you go girl. I'm so proud of you!"

She smiles. "Thanks, Isla."

I spot my next victim out of the corner of my eye, hovering near Elise and Aisha. She avoids my gaze, until I call her name out.

"Oh, hi," Lucy says.

"Thanks for coming."

"Yeah, whatever."

"I got the idea of this club from you."

"Huh?" She acts nonchalant, but a light pink flush covers her cheeks.

"Well, I've got to go and make my speech."

"Okay."

I'm not naive enough to think that Lucy and I will ever be friends, and that's perfectly fine. We don't have to be friends to understand each other's problems and support each other.

The chatter has pretty much died down by now so I am forced to begin my speech.

"Hi, guys." I wave and everyone greets me back, which helps build my confidence a little. And by little, I mean a very miniscule, tiny amount. I'm still super freaking nervous. "Umm, well I'm Isla Wu. If you didn't know me, now you do." I chuckle nervously. "Ah."

But after fumbling through the introduction, the talking becomes more natural and I really do start to understand what they mean when they talk about speaking from the heart. "I went through a mental breakdown last semester which caused me to fail all of my classes. I thought there wasn't anyone that I could turn to in order to talk about my problems, but I understand now that it was the most incorrect mindset. In light of my experiences, I decided to make this club where we can talk to each other and be each other's support systems. Umm, so yeah."

I close my eyes, expecting to meet utter humiliation. Instead, I'm greeted with standing ovations and big smiles. Clapping the loudest are Slater and Raina. When the claps cease, I start a group introduction activity that I hope no one finds to be awkward and embarrassing. It's a weird trust exercise where everyone gets paired into groups to solve a problem.

No one says anything, though, so either they didn't think it was terrible or they're going to gossip about me later, but you know what? I don't care.

By the end of the meeting, a genuine surge of happiness settles within me. I think I conveyed my points well and potentially created a community where we can all support each other. I might be a little too optimistic and starry eyed right now, but whatever. The cynicism can come later.

Raina gives me a huge hug. "You were so great up there!"

"That means the world." I beam. "Did I come on a little too strong?"

"No, it was awesome. You were awesome.," Raina gives me one more hug. Before she walks out the classroom, she gives a subtle point with her head towards Slater and winks at me. I roll my eyes.

Classic Raina.

"I'm so in awe of you." Slater kisses me on the forehead. "You killed it."

"I love you." I don't think I'll ever get tired of telling him.

"I love you, too." He slings an arm around my shoulder as we walk. "Hey, why does Raina keep wiggling her eyebrows at me and calling me "nerd"?"

My laughter echoes down the empty hallway. "I told her about the book."

He starts laughing, too. "No wonder."

"Hey, I think it's cute. I have to admit, I love nerds. What's the next book you're annotating for me?"

"That's my little secret." Slater winks at me before leaning over to kiss me.

And I can finally say that I am okay.

CHECK OUT THESE OTHER GREAT READS FROM ROWAN PROSE

Ellen Zheng is an avid lover of books that make her cry and Taylor Swift songs. As the child of immigrant parents, she wanted to implement her experiences and culture into her writing, especially mental health. Through channels such as literature and entertainment, she believes we can work on destigmatizing mental health and convey that people don't have to suffer alone. She is a debut author of young adult fiction and resides in Georgia.